Blood Moon

By Barry Joyce

This is entirely a work of fiction. No person, place or organisation bears anything but a tenuous relationship with reality.

Copyright © 2016 B V Joyce

All rights reserved. This book or any part thereof may not be reproduced in any form without the author's previous consent.

For my dear wife, Victoria

Chapter 1

Angie was not with me that day. It was just as well. I had screwed up – big time.

I still find it difficult to believe how poorly I had prepared for that fateful meeting with Otto. As a direct result, my cover was blown and this had inevitably led to my seizure, and to the dire situation in which I now found myself.

Whirr-u-whirr. There it was again – louder this time. A train was on its way, thundering towards me as I lay on the track. My state of anxiety, already so high, ratcheted up yet another notch and I once again tested the complex system of tethers that held me firmly between the rails.

I was not entirely immobilised. There was a good degree of play. I could freely move a hand or a foot, but each such movement produced an equal and opposite effect on another part of my body. However I moved, one or other limb would always extend completely over one of the rails. The fiendish Baron had concocted a cat's cradle of ropes that allowed me the choice of limb to be amputated.

Whirr-u-whirr. Much closer now, and I could hear the clatter of the wheels on the track. My head and body would surely pass underneath the train. But could I survive? Would some protruding item of the rolling stock scoop me up? Would the rush of air swivel my body under the wheels? Could I bear the terrible shock as my limb was severed?

But which limb? I had only seconds to choose now. My left hand – I decided my left hand was the one to be sacrificed. To select it, I tugged my right foot off one rail, whereupon my left hand and forearm stretched out above my head and over the opposite rail. The sweat was pouring off me as I waited, terrified. The noise was thunderous now. How many seconds to impact? I started to count. One, two, three ...

The train hit. I screamed and tried to sit up. But my severed hand was useless and I fell back onto the bed, hot and covered in sweat. Angie turned towards me.

"What the hell are you doing?" She cried.

"My hand doesn't work," I answered limply.

I brought my right hand over to examine the stump on the left and was surprised to feel it still in position. But I couldn't lift it. I picked it up and let it flop onto the bed. It was useless.

"My hand is paralysed," I said.

"Don't be ridiculous."

"It is," I insisted, "I can't move it. And I can't feel anything with it either."

"You've slept on it," she murmured, as she once again turned her back to me. "Just leave it alone. It'll come back in a moment."

I waited, apprehensive.

I frequently dream at night. Sometimes the dreams involve people I know; at other times, they are populated by strangers. Some are self-contained, whilst others arrive as a series of linked episodes. On most occasions, I recall the details later in the day but occasionally, as on that day, I wake up at some dramatic point.

The use and feeling of my hand did return very gradually. She was right, dammit. I acknowledged her correct diagnosis, not explicitly in words, but by waving my hand around in extravagant gestures. She failed to see this, and continued to doze with her back towards me.

But she was right again. She was always right. At least, that is what she constantly claimed. And she probably believed it too. Like many mornings, this was not a good start to the day. Our relationship had waned over the last few years. We had been together for less than ten of them, but it sometimes felt more like a marriage of thirty years or more. We remained on friendly terms, but the magic spark had all but disappeared.

We no longer took every opportunity to make a grab for each other's body as we once did. We made love still – on occasion. Or rather, we had sex. But it had become a mere physical, almost a mechanical, activity, and I am uncertain how much love was still involved. We still cared for each other, but love – I'm not sure. Love is difficult to define. Lust is much easier.

We had met just over nine years earlier, on a tube train heading for Hammersmith. There had been a long wait, and the train was very crowded. She was very short and my first view of her was a mass of dark brown curly hair as her face pressed up against my chest. As I sensed her look up, I folded my chin into my neck to look down at her. She had a sweet elfin face, and I made some crass remarks about the quality of the view "down there". She smiled, but then looked down once more into my chest.

Many of the passengers got out at the next station, and I should have been one of them. But I stayed on and was able to study her more closely. Such snatched inspections are necessarily short, un-detailed affairs so as not to embarrass or become embarrassed oneself. But it was enough to reveal that her elfin face contained all the elfin features that it should, and a quick scan of her body revealed a neat petite frame, albeit with a chest that appeared to be somewhat flatter than I would have wished.

Nevertheless, I was certainly attracted to her and summoned up sufficient courage to ask her how far she was going.

"To the end," she answered lightly.

"Oh! I'm going to Hammersmith too," I lied. Then after a pause I added, "Have you had a good day?"

She made no reply for a moment or two but then, with a slight shrug, she said simply, "The usual."

This led to some stilted probing about her work as a secretary, and then on to other equally dull topics, such as crowded trains and the weather. This sort of opening seems to be almost obligatory but immediately sets up an obstacle that one has to overcome with care. I knew of several pubs around Hammersmith station and lied once more to the effect that I usually called in for a pint – to separate my work and leisure lives. Would she join me?

Again, there were some moments of hesitation. She looked me up and down and, presumably deciding that I was sufficiently presentable, or at the very least would pose no threat of physical harm, she surprised me by taking my arm with a cheery, "OK."

The rest, I suppose, could be described as history. But after nine years, I would better describe it as ancient history. The intervening years passed happily enough but perhaps lacked the necessary innovation and excitement that maintains the momentum of a relationship. This was due in no small measure to our work, which kept us apart for long periods over the years. Angie lifted herself out of her previous dull work and managed to gain a demanding position as a Personal Assistant to an international tycoon of some sort, a job she loved but that involved both odd and long hours, along with frequent overseas trips.

Although entirely based in England, my hours too had also been long and varied. I had entered the world of property development, both commercial and residential, and it had gone well. I threw my lot in with a friend from my schooldays who had some degree of training and experience, and we worked famously together until he was tragically killed when a scaffold collapsed on one of our sites. I had by then gained considerable familiarity with finance, planning and building practises, all of which seemed entirely logical and came naturally to me so that I was able to continue on my own account. Looking back, I was probably extremely lucky, but at the time I felt that I achieved my success through long sweaty hours of toil on site followed by equally long sweaty hours of worry at night. I was proud of what I had accomplished and had amassed a considerable fortune, which I had invested, partly in property, but also in a variety of traditional savings products.

Angie turned in the bed, yawned and stretched her arms up above her head. The bedclothes receded to her waist revealing her meagre breasts, which had never had the opportunity of bulking up with babies' milk. This lack of any family had never been a contentious matter between us. In the early days, of course, we had discussed it frequently and at considerable length, but thereafter we had persistently put our work first. It was only now, in our early thirties and with our future financially secure, that the chance of starting a family would seem to be a practical proposition. But any talk on the subject had long since dried up. Although not exactly running out of time yet, Angie would have to give the matter serious consideration over the next few years but for the moment, she remained wedded to her work more than to me, let alone any thoughts of a baby.

She threw back the bedclothes and padded into the makeshift bathroom area I had formed alongside the bedroom. There was no hot water in those days. The shower was still on the outside, fed by a hose ranged back and forth across the south-facing wall. This provided sufficient hot water for us to have a shower at night – at least if you were female, and therefore had claim to the first shower. I always had to hurry with mine if I was to avoid a cold finish. Constant hot water was now high on my list of projects, but it was early summer in Italy ... and hot.

I waited patiently for my turn at the basin, listening to all the little personal noises of her morning ablutions. They were always the same and I mentally ticked them off – like a checklist, a countdown to my routine commencing.

I am still not entirely certain how we ended up in Italy, for neither of us speaks the language. I had successfully completed a large and very profitable project and needed a change and a rest. The idea of buying a property abroad beckoned as a suitable adventure, but I suspect that it was also subconsciously an attempt to breathe some life back into our marriage.

"How about buying a place abroad – somewhere in the sun?" I suggested one day.

"What a great idea," Angie responded immediately. She threw herself into the project with enthusiasm, and it immediately became wholeheartedly a joint venture.

We started our search in France. It seemed the obvious choice and I had given very little thought to anywhere else. But after much internet searching and a couple of unsuccessful forays, Angie remembered a holiday she had spent in Italy as a new teenager. The memories swirled around in her mind for several days before she gave me some glowing accounts of it, and announced that she would like to investigate what that country had to offer. The best part of twenty years had passed and she had little idea where they had holidayed, but she recalled it as a land full of wooded hills and lakes. This suggested the north of Italy and, with the high prices asked for anything around the large popular lakes, we concentrated our search around some of the smaller ones.

On our very first tour, we were fortunate to come across a somewhat dilapidated farmhouse set amongst a wooded hillside that led down to a quiet lake. It was structurally sound, but in desperate need of a great deal of loving attention – something I had both the time and the desire to lavish upon it. We made our decision on the spot and set the legal formalities in motion before we left. These took an inordinate amount of time and set us to wonder what we had taken on. But in the fullness of time, it did finally belong to us, and we were able to begin work. After the initial clean-up, I spent long periods out there tackling the necessary structural work, with Angie joining me whenever her job allowed her to grab a week or so.

This had been just such a visit, and it was Angie's last day. On the drive to Bergamo airport, we fell into a heated argument about the continued lack of hot water.

"You've had plenty of time to get it done," she insisted, and then finally, "I warn you, I'm not coming out again until it's sorted."

After this outburst, we talked little for the rest of the journey, so I was able to spend the time working up a mental list of equipment I would need. These materials are not readily available in our neighbourhood and, as soon as I had waved Angie into security, I went in search of a suitable plumbing store. By the time I left, the car was brimmed to the roof with copper – a large storage cylinder, lengths of pipe, and plastic bags full of joints, bends and other gear. About halfway home, I stopped off at a roadside restaurant for an early evening meal. My accomplishments as a cook are extremely limited and I take every opportunity to avoid eating the results.

I woke early the following morning to another bright day and decided to make an immediate start. It was going to get very hot later.

I have no formal training as a plumber, but my work has provided me with a good knowledge of most building trades. I had already carried out much of the preparation, so work progressed swiftly. By noon, the storage tank was operational, and by mid-afternoon, the shower was connected and the enclosure ready for tiling. It had already been a long day, and the work had been in awkward and constricted areas. My body ached and I felt exhausted. I needed a break.

For the last hour or so, I had been hallucinating about swimming in cool water, and I decided to drive down to the lake. A narrow, twisty road leads to a small village, which has no shop but does possess a friendly little bar and restaurant where we had already spent many happy hours. A hundred metres or so beyond the last house lies a recreation area with swings and a roundabout for children, along with a small section set aside for camping, albeit with very limited facilities. Between these two areas, a rough patch of ground provides parking for half a dozen cars. This was empty as I arrived and I was able to park right up to the grass that leads down to the water's edge, where the ground becomes a gently shelving slope of mud and small stones.

With no one around, it was easy to strip down to the swim shorts I had put on back at the house. Not being a very trusting soul, I locked my clothes away out of sight in the boot, along with my mobile and some loose change that I keep in an emergency wallet. Padding around in bare feet, I locked the car, tucked the key into the button-down pocket of my swimmers and headed for the water. The soft mud squelched its way between my toes as I waded out, slowly at first but gaining momentum in readiness to dive. At this time of year, the water has not yet enjoyed sufficient sun to warm it to any great degree, but this was just what my hot and slightly sweaty body needed. I swam out for about a hundred metres and turned on my back, floating for a while. Bliss...

After a few minutes, I began to swim along the centre of the lake, sometimes using breaststroke, others a relaxed crawl. The difference in temperatures between the water and my body soon equalised and I began to feel more comfortable, enjoying the exercise.

I must have swum for twenty minutes or more without paying much attention to my surroundings. I did not feel particularly tired, but it slowly dawned on me that I was now in a sector of the lake unknown to me, and with a good distance to swim back. I trod water for a while and looked around at the new scenery. Much of it was very similar to the area I knew, but it was somewhat wilder. Then, a couple of hundred yards in front of me I spotted a small island close to the far bank. But what took my attention was the fact that it appeared to be inhabited.

I made the fateful decision then, that I would set myself a target. I would swim around the island and only then make my way back to the car.

As I approached, I realised that the lake must have widened out at this point since there was a considerable distance between the far shore and the island – I estimated more than a hundred metres of clear water. The island was largely wooded, but a clearing had been formed at the southern end on which stood the house that I had seen. It was not a new house, but neither was it very old, built in the vernacular style of the region. It was not particularly large, but it did reflect a certain aura of elegance.

As I got nearer, set somewhat lower than the house itself, I could make out a paved area from which a couple of glinting steel posts erupted, suggesting that it probably contained a swimming pool. And on this terrace, lounging on a sunbed, my eyes settled on a figure, the girl who was to dominate my life for many of the coming months.

Chapter 2

At that distance, and partly because she was holding up a magazine, I could make out neither her age nor many of the features of her face or body. She did not hear my unusual form of arrival, and I decided that it would be rude to announce it by calling out. I resolved to stick to my plan and set off to circle the island. Almost immediately, I came across a wooden landing approached by wide concrete steps leading up from the water. A stone paved path then led up towards the house. At the far side of this landing was a wooden hut at water level, which I assumed would house a boat of some sort. I swam on past this, where the uninviting rocky banks of the island's shore rose steeply to a densely wooded interior. It was at least another ten minutes before I arrived back in front of the house.

I have no idea what caused her to look up that day, Signora or Signorina – I was still not sure. But I saw her suddenly draw aside the magazine and look out at me. I thought I perceived a small smile but, more certainly, I saw her lift her right arm and waggle her hand in a cheery wave. I returned her wave and may have continued to tread water and stare a moment too long, for she suddenly sprang upright on the lounger, clutching the magazine to what I guessed would be her naked chest. She beckoned to me and followed this immediately by pointing in the direction of the landing stage. It was a clear invitation to visit, so unexpected that it set my mind in a whirl.

Both my conservative upbringing and my natural shyness screamed at me to wave once more and then to turn and head back. I was undressed and a long way from home, and feeling more than a little vulnerable. I raised my arm for that goodbye wave, but it had gained a life of its own and continued to arch over and then plough back into the water in a lazy front crawl, heading for the steps.

The concrete was slippery where it was underwater, but I was soon up onto firm dry slabs. I half expected her to greet me somewhere along the path up to the house, but there was no sign of anyone as I made my way around the side. Here, the ways are separated. To the left, the path continued for a short distance, framed by colourful flowerbeds, before a flight of steps led straight up to the house. I continued, however, where the path gradually widened out into a terrace, constructed of the same stone slabs.

And there she was, on the far side of a small pool.

I remember that my immediate feeling was one of disappointment as I perceived that both halves of her bikini were now firmly in place. This was odd since, had they not been, I would have had considerable difficulty knowing where to put my eyes. She had hauled herself up on the lounger with her back almost vertical, and her face wore a warm smile of welcome. My nervousness returned as I skirted the pool and approached her with as much confidence as I could muster.

She was still smiling as she held out her hand. "Selene," she announced.

"Martin," I replied as I leant over for a fleeting handshake.

"Would you care to dry yourself off, Martin?" she asked in a light, cheery English voice. "There are some towels in the back," she added, pointing behind her.

Was she really English, I wondered as I gratefully accepted the invitation which allowed me to break the tension of the meeting of our eyes. "Thanks," I said and turned to find a stone pool house built into a bank that rose sharply up to the tree line. Inside the open door, there was a shower cubicle and toilet, along with a wide built-in cupboard with hanging space, drawers and cubbyholes. These were all stacked with a good selection of deep-pile bathrobes, fluffy towels and a basket filled with flippers, goggles, balls and other articles for water play.

I grabbed one of the towels and started back, drying my hair. For a while, I was able to study Selene out of her view, first from the back, then from the side. As I approached, I could continue the examination surreptitiously with judicious use of the towel as I dried off the rest of my body. What lay in front of me both excited and frightened me in equal measure. Never in my life had I stood before such a beautiful woman – truly a goddess. If such a portrayal may seem excessive, I can think of no better word to describe the devotion that my infatuation with her was to induce.

At this point, I find myself somewhat at a loss to know how to proceed. Somehow, I have to convey to you how, in the course of this one short day, I was to become totally obsessed with her. As always, it began with physical attraction. Every man has a different idea of his ideal woman. It is a popular belief that either legs or breasts initially attract a man, but this is far too simplistic. Eyes, teeth, hair, and just about every other feature have their devotees and I seriously considered whether to leave you to picture Selene as your own vision.

However, even though this was more than a year ago now, I can recall with great precision how my eyes first perceived her. My mind very quickly pieced together the jigsaw of the various pieces – the fleeting glimpses tucked away as I approached, and I will attempt to describe the picture that emerged.

If such a description would normally proceed from head to toe, I remember the picture in reverse order – that in which I first set eyes upon it as I emerged from the pool house. In full complement, the toes were conspicuous, painted in a shade somewhere between pink and red. But it was her long shapely legs that immediately drew the attention of my eyes. A light golden tan from the early summer sun set off their perfect curves as she lay on a thick plain yellow mattress. They were silky smooth and glistened slightly from the remains of some tanning lotion. Her hips, modestly sheathed in a bright red satin-like material, splayed inwards to a narrow waist, and then out again to the swell of her bikini top. There was no loose spilling of her breasts outside it – full but firm, I remember guessing.

It is difficult to describe the face that emerged from a fine slim neck without some hackneyed form of expression – that of an angel perhaps, or one capable of launching a thousand ships. It was almond-shaped, with high cheekbones, a generous wide mouth, and a cheeky little nose – slightly upturned. But if anything trumped her legs, it was her eyes. They were simply staggering. The irises were blue – not a deep blue, but the pale blue of a lazy summer afternoon sky. They were jewelled islands in the sea of the whites that surrounded them – twinkling brightly.

A mass of light golden hair topped off this stunning vision. It cascaded in loose curls around her face, even as her head lay against the back of the lounger. I could make out no signs of darker roots, and remember wondering if this was her natural colour.

By this time, I was approaching the foot of her lounger, still mussing my hair with the towel. "Pull up another sunbed," she suggested. Looking around, there were a couple more scattered over the terrace and I brought one of them up close to the right of her.

"Well, Mr Swimmer, what brings you to my island?"

I snorted a short laugh. "I've been working all day, and got very hot and ..." I paused briefly with the word "sweaty" hovering on my lips, but I thought it might paint the wrong picture so I quickly continued "... and thought a swim would cool me down."

"Did you swim over from the landing stage?"

I had swum to the landing stage, not from it. What did she mean? But, of course, there had to be a corresponding stage on the far bank. "Oh," I said. "No. To be honest, I didn't notice any landing on the shore."

"It's not easy to spot now. The trees around it have become a bit overgrown," she said. "Where did you get in then?"

"It was some distance away – round the bend there," I said, pointing in the direction of our village. "I was so enjoying myself, I just kept on going. Then I saw this island, and thought I'd investigate."

"I'm glad you did."

"It's a great place you have here."

"Yes. We love it here."

The "we" punched me in the stomach. I cannot think why I should imagine that such a beautiful creature would be living there alone. But, ridiculously, I felt a stab of jealousy, and it hurt.

Perhaps she read the disappointment in my face, for hers suddenly crinkled into a wide smile. As it did so, I caught a fleeting glimpse of a long, thin scar that ran down most of the left-hand side of her face. It showed up as white against her otherwise golden skin, and the cheek moved a trifle stiffly as she smiled – not quite as it should. Why had I not noticed it before? It was either a very minor wound or some skilful makeup disguised it well. But for rather too long, I could not take my eyes away from it.

"You don't live here permanently." A question rather than a statement was asked quickly to cover my embarrassment.

"Good heavens, no. We rent it. I move about quite a bit. I suppose, if I have a home anywhere, it's back in England – where I grew up."

I had been a trifle unnerved by the discovery of the scar, but the opening conversation had been convivial enough and I was already feeling sufficiently confident to shake it off. And in some weird way, the fact that I had hit upon this slight blemish added to that confidence. No longer was she total perfection. Perhaps – just maybe – she was not so far out of my league after all.

Out of my league? What on earth was I thinking of? What did I want of her? Was it purely sexual? The sight of a beautiful woman unsurprisingly raises my natural desires, and this one possessed such beauty in abundance. It would surely be entirely natural to fantasise about making love to her sometime soon. I make no apologies for this. I am a man.

But more than this, there was already something else, something deeper, more honourable somehow – simply to spend time with her, to talk with her, to learn of her thoughts, her attitudes, her likes and dislikes.

I have described Selene's physical appearance at some length, for I believe you must have a clear picture of her. If she sounds too perfect to be true, then I agree. But that is exactly how I saw her on that first meeting, and it was daunting. My own looks, although I am assured that they are by no means gruesome, are comparatively unimportant.

Some side attractions, grace notes if you like, further guaranteed the surrender of my heart as the day unfolded. The perfect set of teeth set wide in a generous mouth as her lips parted in a smile, the clear bell-like sound that rang out with her joyful laugh, and the occasional uninhibited toss of her hair to re-order a stray curl.

And then there was her voice. Before that day, I do not believe it ever crossed my mind that vocal cords could play any part in sexual attraction. But there it was – openly, almost brazenly. It had all the confidence of breeding and good education but with no hint of the tiresome affectations of certain sets of the upper class. It was light and clear, coloured by highlights fashioned from the same bell that inhabited her laugh.

"Are you married?" she asked suddenly.

It was a direct question, out of the blue, one I had not anticipated – at least, not yet. I was wrong-footed, confused and could only manage a muted, "Yes".

I regretted it immediately. Surely, I should have drawn a less joyous picture by adding, "but my wife doesn't understand me" or even, "but we're separated"? But these all sounded too hackneyed and I eventually settled for a simple, "She's back in England," and countered with, "You?"

"No. Not now." I decided it was too early to press her further than she wished to volunteer.

"How long have you been here?" I asked.

"This time?" She hesitated. "About ten days."

"It's a regular haunt then?"

"Yes. I love it. It's such a contrast to my normal life, so restful, so peaceful – just the occasional guy swimming by."

I smiled. "Does that happen often?"

"First time. Strange that ..." I melted in her smile.

I wondered whether the change from "we love it" to "I love it" held any significance. Had she noticed my hesitation and was attempting to put me more at ease?

"Selene," I mused. "It's a pretty name, but unusual. I've never heard it before. Is it English?"

"Not normally – no. My mother was Greek. She was a film star ... quite famous for a while in Greece. She had me when she was very young. I never knew my real father. Later, she married a rich Englishman who forced her to give up acting. He was jealous. Not a nice man." She paused for a few moments, recollecting something from her past. "In fact, he's a horrid beast of a man. I hate him."

"I'm sorry. That can't have made for a very happy childhood."

"No," she said simply.

It was the first time I had seen her in a serious mood, clearly caused by memories of dark places, and I moved swiftly to change it.

"Did you follow her into show business?"

"Hmm," she smiled. Her mood had seemingly passed quickly enough. "I did for a bit. My mother managed to get me into drama school, and I did get a few parts. When she died, I got by with that and a bit of modelling work. But by then I was part of what they used to call the "jet set" – you know, horse racing, power boats, fast cars ..." her voice tailed off and once again any trace of a smile vanished from her face. Was she saddened by thoughts of a past world, perhaps no longer available to her?

But again, the mood evaporated as quickly as it had arrived.

"So," she began. "What brings you to these parts?"

"Oh well, things were getting a bit stale at home," I ventured, in an attempt to soften the picture of married bliss. "We needed a new project of some sort. I wanted a break from work, and I'd saved some money, so we decided to look for a holiday home to buy – somewhere in Europe. Eventually, we came across this little spot, just around that bend, on the opposite bank. It's higher up in the hills, in the woods, all by itself. There's nothing much around it – just a small hamlet down by the lake." Then after a short pause, "It needs a lot of work though."

"What are you going to do with it? Does it need enlarging?"

She was showing interest with some enthusiasm, and I gave her a rundown of all we had done so far and our proposals for the future. The last thing I wanted to do was to bore her, so I kept it brief.

"That sounds good. I'd love to see it," she said, and then as an afterthought, "I know a good local builder if you need one."

"I'll be doing most of the work myself," I said. "I can put my hand to most things."

"What a useful man to know," she announced with one of those delightful twinkles in her eye. Was she flirting, I wondered. Was it possible?

But the moment was gone in an instant, as the figure of a man appeared at the top of the steps that led down from the house.

Chapter 3

He was carrying a silver tray covered with a couple of glasses and a variety of bottles. From behind him, a dog appeared, yawned, stretched and slowly followed him down the steps. It was a large dog with long hair, almost white, and big floppy ears. I know little about dogs, not even liking them very much, but I guess that it was some sort of sheep dog. It wandered slowly over to Selene's proffered hand, giving it a couple of licks before settling down on the terrace at the foot of her lounger. "This is Lucio," she announced, introducing the dog rather than the man.

      As he approached, Selene did not look at him. Quite to the contrary, I felt that her eyes were on me – studying me intently. I did not turn to meet her gaze but kept my eyes on this unwanted arrival. He was a big man, tall and muscular, with the sort of muscles that can only be developed by long hours in the gym. His face was interesting rather than classically handsome – a typically swarthy Italian face, dark eyes, jet-black hair and a dense rash of matching stubble that partly obscured a rather too prominent chin. As he reached the terrace, he placed the tray down on a wooden table that stood against the pool house wall. He picked up a large straight-sided glass filled with a clear liquid, a couple of cubes of ice and two thick slices of what looked to be lime. It was to be later, much later, that I was to learn that her favoured drink was vodka and tonic.

Without a word, he brought it over and placed it on a small wooden table that already lay to the left of Selene.

"This is my man," she announced briefly.

"*Your man?*" I queried.

She said nothing for a few seconds. Then, refusing to elaborate further, she continued, "His name is Pino."

I glanced up at him and said, "Hi."

He acknowledged me with a stiff nod of the head, and then asked with a strong Italian accent, "What drink you want?"

"Drinks?" I exclaimed. "What time is it? I haven't got my watch on ..."

"About half past six," announced Selene, after a brief look at a small but expensive-looking gold watch that dangled loosely from her slim wrist.

"Good heavens! I must be going soon. The sun will be gone before long, and I've got quite a swim in front of me."

"Come on. Stay for a while longer. What would you like to drink?"

I hesitated, but then, "OK ... gin and tonic?" I queried Pino.

"Si," he confirmed. "Lemon or lime?"

"Lemon, please."

Pino returned to his tray, mixed my drink, and brought it over along with a twin of her side table. And then Selene's man was gone – at least, for the time being.

What did she mean – my man? I had been straining for clues ever since she had first used the expression. I had detected no sign of any chemistry between them. Indeed, she had almost totally ignored him, failing even to thank him for her drink. For his part, he had seemed blandly servile, just doing his job. I decided that he was most probably a local, perhaps employed as part of the rental arrangement to look after the needs of the house's occupants. It must be her term for a servant.

"You were telling me about your little house," she revived our earlier conversation, without elaborating further on her man. "How long is it going to take you to put to rights?"

"Oh, I don't know. It depends on how long I can spend over here – probably about a year. There's quite a bit to do."

We talked of the local area, of which she seemed to know very little. Angie and I had explored more of the region than she had during her numerous visits. This gave me an idea, and I suggested we should explore the lake together and was encouraged when she leapt at the suggestion.

"That sounds great, Martin. We'll take the boat out tomorrow. I'll organise a picnic and we'll spend the day exploring the whole lake."

"It's a date," I agreed happily.

Selene went on to talk of areas she knew better. Her normal stamping ground was further south – Rome, Capri, and the Italian Riviera. Just as she would be in England for Ascot, Henley and the Wimbledon fortnight, so she would visit these places in their respective seasons. I knew very little of these, of course – and then only by repute. She was a good listener, but an even better raconteur, and she kept me entertained with stories of the high life. But never did they throw any real light on her private life. How she lived. How she loved.

An hour or more passed, with the sun disappearing behind the hills without us noticing. But a sudden slight chill brought pressing matters to the fore.

"I have to be going," I announced, looking pointlessly at my bare left wrist.

"That's silly," Selene declared. "It'll be dark before long. You could get lost. It might be dangerous. You might drown." And then, "We can put you up for the night. My man will be down soon. He'll be making dinner right now, and I'm sure he'll be able to rustle up enough for an extra one."

Everything shouted loudly at me to say, "No, thank you", and to get going. I struggled to think of the implications of my domestic responsibilities. Tiling the shower could wait, of course, but what about my car stuck out in the countryside? My mobile was locked in the boot and Angie would be phoning to let me know that she had returned home safely. She would continue to phone until she got a reply – throughout the night if necessary. How would I explain my absence? And had I secured the house properly when I left for an intended short swim?

"But I've got no clothes," was the only limp excuse I could summon up.

She laughed briefly, "That doesn't matter. We can fix you up with something." After a moment's thought, she hit on the solution, "Fetch one of the bathrobes from the poolroom."

As Pino appeared once more on the steps, I went into the pool house and tried on a couple of bathrobes, eventually finding one that fitted pretty well. I kept on my swimming shorts, which by now were completely dry, and checked myself in the full-length mirror on the wall. Not too bad, I said to myself.

When I emerged, Pino was approaching Selene's lounger. All of a sudden, I was amazed to see him bend down and force his right hand under Selene's knees and the other behind her waist. Slowly, but with considerable ease, he lifted her off the sunbed. With a slight bump of readjustment, he started carrying off my new goddess. As I watched all this unfold, I felt my jaw drop and my mouth hang open. I hoped I was wrong, and that I didn't look too stupid, for I was aware that Selene was still looking at me with a slight smile on her face, all the while watching my reactions.

I stood there, numb, rooted to the spot as Pino carried her to a wheelchair by the wall. Either I had not noticed it earlier or he had pulled it out from somewhere. As he gently lowered her into the chair, Selene yelled out to me as if nothing had occurred, "You go up the stairs, Martin. We'll see you at the top."

"Right," was all I could manage as they set off up a path that took a circuitous route, without any steps. Lucio lazily unfurled himself from his slumber and followed them.

My mind was still racing as I reached the top and waited for them on a smaller terrace that looked out over the lake. She was still looking at me and smiling as Pino wheeled her past me and into the house through open french doors.

The large room we entered was simply but elegantly furnished. On the far side, a comfortable sitting area was ranged around a wood-burning stove, unlit for now, along with a sizeable TV. Just inside the open french doors was a large oak table that would comfortably seat eight diners, but tonight was set for just two. Pino pushed Selene up to the table and I nervously took the place opposite. He then vanished into the kitchen and for a few moments, we sat looking at each other in silence.

"There's an elephant in the room," Selene announced.

I remained lost for words and stayed silent.

"Come on," she continued. "Let's get it out of the way. You want to know what happened to me. Yes?"

"I'm so sorry," I said feebly.

"Don't be," she cut in quickly. "I'm OK. It's a long time ago now."

She paused then, but I decided that I should let her talk.

"I could make it a long tale," she began. "But the details are just too boring. I was in a car accident. It damaged my spinal cord. My husband was driving much too fast – and much too drunk. I'm lucky to be alive." After a short pause, she added, "He didn't have the same good fortune ..."

"I'm so sorry," I said again.

Selene said nothing. She just pursed her beautiful full lips and nodded. The elephant may have been banished, but it had left a sizeable shadow in the room.

After a moment's awkward silence, she added, "So – that's it. For the last five years, I've had no use of my legs."

"That's criminal, "I ventured. "They are so beautiful."

"Are you flirting with me, young man?"

"I believe I might be." Amazingly, I was feeling bolder.

Selene threw her head back and laughed – that easy bell-like laugh that had already captivated me. At the same time, she reached out and placed her hand on mine. It was like an electric shock, and I found it difficult not to withdraw it. But it must have lit up my face, and I beamed a smile back at her.

Pino entered carrying a bottle of Pinot Grigio in a terracotta cooler, which he placed in the centre of the table and disappeared again. "Pour us some wine, Martin," Selene invited. I had only just half-filled the two elegant glasses when Pino returned and placed a plate of cold chicken salad in front of each of us.

"It won't be a feast, I'm afraid," Selene apologised. "I don't eat very much at night."

As Pino once again disappeared into the kitchen, she leaned forward across the table and said in a low conspiratorial whisper, "Pino's not a great cook, and he's got very little imagination."

"It'll do me fine," I whispered back. "From what I can see, he's got more skill in the kitchen than I have."

The exchange was nothing really, but we had swapped small secrets, and that gave me further encouragement. Thus emboldened, I thought I would try to winkle out a bit more information.

"Does Pino come with the house?"

"Hardly – no. He's my man." There it was again. How very annoying. I was no further on. He cooked for her and seemed to be of general help around the house.

But I now knew she was disabled, and this led me to speculate that he may be a professional carer – some sort of nurse perhaps. She was unwilling to elaborate further, however, and I decided to change tack.

"You said that "we" rented the house. I assume you don't mean you and Pino?"

"You're fishing still," she accused, with a wicked smile on her face. She had caught me out, and I could feel my face begin to flush. She seemed to like this and continued, "I will answer your question though. It's my agent, back in England. He arranges things like this for me. OK?"

"Sure," I said, a little shame faced. "I'm just fascinated to find out a little more about you ..."

"I'm sure," she accepted, with the same mischievous grin. After a pause, she continued, "Tell me more about yourself though – your marriage. Do you have children?"

"No." I was relieved that I could assure her of this without lying. "We both got too involved with our work – never got round to it somehow. And now ..." I paused for a second or two before I continued, "well ... I think I mentioned we're having problems. Having kids is no solution. I'm sure both Angie and I are agreed on that."

"Pity," she said, "I'm sure you'd make a great dad."

"Maybe. I'm certainly fond of kids."

The conversation flowed easily that evening. It continued to be mildly flirtatious, with neither of us wanting to give away too much information without getting something in return – teasingly competitive. We found that we had much in common, but there were also considerable differences – particularly in our respective backgrounds and lifestyles. Throughout her life, Selene had moved in circles that I had only read about or seen in films, and I was fascinated to hear her stories, both comical and sad, about life in the fast lane.

Pino entered the room, and the distraction caused me to look again for the watch on my empty wrist. Selene smiled and looked at hers. "It's half past ten," she announced.

"È ora di andare a letto." Pino said quietly to Selene.

"Pino says it's bedtime," she translated, looking at me.

There seemed to be no room for argument as Pino began to push her chair towards a corridor that led off between the kitchen and dining areas, evidently to the sleeping quarters. I got up and followed, somewhat annoyed that my evening with her was to be terminated so abruptly.

Two doors led off the corridor, almost opposite each other. As Pino began to push Selene through the right-hand door, she suddenly stopped the wheelchair using the manual control wheel and skilfully turned it around to face me. She pointed to the other door, which was already wide open.

"That's your room, Martin. I hope you'll be comfortable."

She seemed to study my face briefly and then, with one of those playful smiles on her lips, she uttered the words that I was to conjure with until the moment I found sleep.

"Good night Martin," she said, and after a short pause continued, "You know, it's only my legs that are useless. The rest of me is intact and in full working order."

I just stared at her, letting her words filter through my brain. But Pino had wheeled her round and was pushing the wheelchair through the door. As he slowly closed the door behind the two of them, he looked at me briefly. Was it a smirk on his face? The look seemed to say, "Make what you can of that, boy." But had he understood? Did he have sufficient English to fully comprehend what she had said? I doubted it somehow.

I stood still for a while, staring at the closed door, and then turned and went into my room. Like the living room, it was sparsely furnished with a standard-size double bed, a small wardrobe and a simple chair. An archway to the far right led through to a small en-suite shower room. I shrugged off the bathrobe and threw it over the back of the chair, following it with my swimsuit. I have always preferred to sleep naked.

Selene's final words were still ringing in my ears. Was it not an invitation to visit her during the night? It certainly sounded like it. But did such offers happen in real life? Was I perhaps in one of my dreams? I pinched myself. "Ouch."

And what of Pino? Was I now occupying his usual room? If so, where would he sleep? Perhaps he normally returned to the mainland for the night. I listened intently but could hear only occasional scuffling noises from the other room.

It was not long before a full day's work and the long swim began to catch up with me, and I fell asleep to the teasing prospect conjured up by Selene's parting words, "The rest of me is intact and in full working order."

Chapter 4

I awoke to a noise from outside the room. Someone was carefully preparing breakfast, trying not to disturb those still in bed. I lay there for a while, listening to cups being lowered gently onto saucers, then got up and went through to the shower room, sloshing some cold water over my face in an attempt to force some life back into my leaden body. With nothing else to wear, I slipped back into my swimsuit and bathrobe.

As I entered the living room, I was surprised to see that Selene was already up, sitting in the same place as the previous evening. She was thumbing through a magazine as she worked her way through a large bowl of cereal. "Good morning," she said brightly.

"Good morning, Selene," I echoed, as I surveyed the room. Lucio was prone again, filling a large basket to the side of the kitchen. He lifted his head briefly to look at me but then, possibly recognising my indifference, closed his eyes once more and tucked it back into his body.

"There'll be some coffee in a moment. What would you like for breakfast? I'll tell Pino."

"I don't have much for breakfast. I'll just have some of that cereal please."

"Oh. You should have more than that, Martin. I'm sure we have some eggs. Or toast, perhaps. It's the best meal of the day. I won't be eating much more until tomorrow."

"No. I'll be fine." I sat down opposite her and poured myself a bowl of cornflakes that were flecked with some suspicious-looking bits.

"I'm so sorry," Selene started. "Last night when we were talking, I forgot that I have to go into town this morning. So we can't go on our trip round the lake."

"That's fine," I said, "I've got some things I really should be getting on with. May I take a rain check though? Make it a date later in the week?"

"Certainly," she agreed enthusiastically. "I'd like that. Now ... I'd better give you my number."

With a decided lack of grace, Pino dumped a pot of coffee on the table, and then pulled a pen from his pocket and threw it down in front of Selene, who gave him a withering glance. His action suggested he had understood our conversation, and I remember wondering if his command of English was better than it appeared.

Selene flipped through her magazine for an empty page and tore off a small strip. After writing her number, she handed it to me, "It's my mobile. There isn't a landline here." I folded it carefully and stuffed it into my swimsuit pocket.

"We've still got a few things to organise before we go," Selene announced. "So why don't you get off when you've finished breakfast? I'll see you another day."

I nodded my acceptance and a moment later, through half a mouthful of milk and cereal, she mumbled, "I'm afraid we can't take you in the boat." She smiled, and added, "So you'll just have to swim."

"That's fine," I said. "No problem."

The conversation failed to flow as it had done the previous evening. Selene seemed preoccupied, perhaps with the thought of her meeting ashore. It was a disappointing form of departure too – no kiss, just a brief handshake and for a moment I wondered whether she was punishing me for my "no show" during the night.

I slipped the bathrobe onto my chair and left through the patio doors. The air was chilly as I scurried down the path to the landing stage, but this was nothing compared with the temperature of the water as I gingerly made my way down the steps into the lake. I took a deep breath and dived in. The leisurely swim of the day before was but a fond memory in this cold water and in less than a quarter of an hour, I was climbing the grassy slope up towards the car. Oddly, it seemed even colder out of the water, and I shivered uncontrollably as I vigorously rubbed myself down with a towel. I remembered that I had tucked a fleece away in the boot of the car for just such an emergency and thankfully zipped myself into it before driving off.

Ten minutes later, I was back in our little house. I changed into my work clothes and hung my swimsuit out to dry in a sunny spot. After another coffee, I began to feel more alive and strong enough to telephone Angie. I had forgotten the hour time difference, and she was still getting ready to leave for work.

"Where the hell were you last night?" was her opening salvo.

"Sorry, darling," I said. "My mobile was dead when I checked it. I set it to charge overnight."

"You can't forget a thing like that, Martin. It's our only means of communication."

"I know. I'm sorry." I changed the subject quickly. "You got home alright then?"

"Yep. It was the usual scrum though. The last thing I wanted was to spend the entire evening trying to get through to you."

"OK. OK. I've said I'm sorry."

"Have you fixed the hot water?"

"I've finished most of the pipework. I'll start on tiling the shower today."

"Good. I've got to get off to work now. Just keep that bloody phone powered up."

"OK. Bye then."

"Bye."

It was not much of a conversation, but I had expected nothing different. My mind turned to the work for the day. Looking over towards the bathroom, I could see the stacks of tiles waiting patiently for me to make a start.

Some men enjoy building walls, and I am one of them. It is a reasonably mechanical process – brick upon brick, stone upon stone, and a satisfying structure slowly but surely emerges. And all the time, the mind is released to wander into any number of nooks and crannies, perhaps addressing some pressing problem in peace and solitude, or maybe just savouring some success or other pleasurable experience. Along with Hadrian, Winston Churchill is probably our history's most famous wall builder, and one can only imagine the ideas that passed through his mind. Fixing tiles offers similar opportunities, but that morning my thoughts remained stubbornly fixed on just one subject. And they were exclusively of Selene.

I feel no need to describe these thoughts. Your imagination is well capable of sparing me that task. Suffice it to say, that morning was the start of a deep longing to be with her. I physically ached to see her again. The urge to telephone her became stronger and stronger until, by the time I had packed up work in the early evening, it had become almost unbearable. But, feeling oddly virtuous in doing so, I managed to resist that urge and decided to leave it for one day. I would telephone her tomorrow.

After microwaving and then eating a rather unappetising frozen meal, I cleaned up the day's building work, prepared it for an early start in the morning, and went to bed. I had been asleep for several hours – I am not sure how many – when I woke abruptly to the sound of someone knocking at the front door. I listened intently and, hearing nothing, dismissed it as a dream and started to doze off once more. But the hammering came again, more insistent now, and I realised that it was real.

Who could it be at this time of night? We did not yet know many people in the area. I threw back the bedclothes, hurriedly put on some pants and a light dressing gown, and went to the door. I had a sudden attack of anxiety for my personal safety as I opened it a crack to peer out. If I had been half expecting a gang of Mafia villains, I could hardly have been more surprised than the sight that greeted me.

"May I come in, Martin?" asked Selene, stepping forward out of the shadows. She was alone, standing unaided on the stone path. Even with the dim light from behind me, I could see that she once again had one of those delightful, but mischievous, smiles on her face.

For several seconds, I was lost for words – quite literally. I could not think of one single word to utter. And when they did finally arrive, they were trite and bore no relationship to all the questions that were exploding in my mind.

"Yes. Come in," was all I could manage as I opened the door wide.

I cannot imagine what I thought would happen next, the unexpected was already happening before my eyes. In the event, Selene calmly stepped over the threshold and walked into the middle of the room. I closed the door and followed her. She turned and, without another word, stepped forward swiftly and threw her arms around my neck. With no answers to any of my silent questions, we spent the next several minutes in a succession of passionate kisses. As I suspected she would be, she was an expert in the art, and this boded well for the lovemaking that I felt sure would follow shortly.

Only a lack of air in our lungs forced us apart. We stood there, panting and flushed, looking at one another and holding hands.

"I owe you an apology," she stated briefly.

"Don't worry," I said. "I enjoyed it."

She laughed. "I do hope so." After a short pause, she continued, "Not that – my legs."

"You'll never need to apologise for them either," I continued, smiling.

"Thank you, kind sir," she said. "But seriously, I do owe you. It was very wrong of me to tease you like that yesterday. It must have been very confusing. Pino was in on the joke, of course, and he's asked me to apologise for him also. He's out in the car – probably asleep again by now."

Once more, I was at a loss as to how to reply. The trick had certainly completely fooled me, but I failed to see it as a joke. It was too sick for my taste, and I felt angry – abused. Eventually, I did manage a wan smile and said stiffly, "OK. You got me."

"You're angry," she said. "I can tell. I have said we're sorry, and I'm prepared to do penance. How can I make it up to you?"

As she said this, she moved up against me and started rubbing her belly against mine. I was aroused immediately and, putting my arms around her began passionately kissing her lips, her face, and her neck. In no time, still locked together, we were shuffling an awkward dance towards the bedroom, all the time undoing and throwing aside pieces of clothing.

Selene's lovemaking was extraordinary. All the skills she had already demonstrated in the passionate kissing that had passed for brief foreplay were extended into the main event. I marvelled at the unexpected strength of her legs, as her heels pressed hard into the small of my back, urging me deeper. It was amazing, overpowering. I found myself unable to control my body and all too soon, I felt the climax approaching until...

... I awoke with a start, bathed in sweat. Pushing back the single sheet, I rolled out of bed and scampered into the bathroom. After splashing cold water over my face and body, I stood there for several minutes with my hands resting on the taps and my head bent, unable to look at myself in the mirror. I felt embarrassed and shameful – dirty somehow. I had let Selene down.

My mood gradually became one of acute disappointment that her visit had been a mere dream and that she was still nothing more than a passing acquaintance. But later, when I had given it further thought, I came to the sad realisation that she was still crippled.

When I had eventually calmed down, I padded back to my bed, where it was a chastened soul that lay wondering whether he would be able to find sleep again. Too often, I have lain awake for hours, my mind picking through a dream in a futile attempt to unravel its secret meaning. Tonight's dream held no such ambiguity, however, and I did manage to fall asleep before too long.

The sun had risen long before me on the following morning. After a quick breakfast, I made a start on finishing the shower. I reckoned I had about half a day's work left to complete it, and it helped to take my mind away from the urge to contact Selene. I continued to be uneasy about the night's dream, but it was today that I had promised myself I would telephone her.

At this thought, my heart missed a beat. Where was her number? Almost immediately, I cursed as I realised that I had failed to rescue the scrap of paper from the pocket of my swimsuit. Feverishly, I retrieved it, fearful that it might have already turned into a useless lump of paper-mâché. It was certainly a mess, but I did manage to prise the folds apart, where I could see that the numbers were very smudged, with some of them having small flakes missing where I had opened it up. I took it inside and very carefully wrote out each digit as best I could make it out. I couldn't be certain, but I convinced myself I had the correct number, which I then entered into my mobile.

I managed to hold off until I took a break in the early afternoon. I rarely get a signal inside the house so I settled myself on the sun-soaked patio and dialled. I was heartened when it seemed to ring, but there was an odd tone, which I failed to recognise, and I tried again in case I had misdialled, but obtained the same result. Exasperated, I forced myself to relax, tucking into a beer and a sandwich.

I telephoned any number of times that afternoon and then well into the evening. Each call ended with the same result and was never diverted to an answering service. I checked the number against Selene's original scrap of paper but could come up with nothing different and went to bed early, feeling very frustrated.

I did not dream again that night, but I did wake up early. I could hear that the good weather had broken, and I lay for a while listening to the rain pattering on the old tiled roof. Unable to regain my sleep, I began to ponder how I was going to make contact with Selene if her mobile remained dead. I could not bear the thought that she would disappear from my life as suddenly as she had entered it.

By now, I had merely to grout the tiles to complete the shower installation. It is a relatively simple, mechanical task but it gave me no satisfaction that morning, and I found myself unable to relax. The work became a chore, an irritating diversion that I had to endure before I could attempt to pick up my embryonic relationship with Selene.

After a hurried lunch, I tried one last time to telephone, but with the same frustrating result. I had no idea how long she was booked to stay on the island and, if I was to have any chance of seeing her again, I realised I would have to pay her another visit.

The rain had stopped, but the sky was still overcast and threatening. Not fancying another long swim, I dug out our local map to plot a route by road. It was immediately clear that to get to the other side of the lake I would need to start in the opposite direction and cross using the narrow road over the dam, further downstream. Still hopeful of meeting up with Selene, I dressed smartly. However, I had no idea how I might contact the house from the lakeside, so I stuffed some swimming gear into the boot.

The journey took longer than I had expected but went without incident. The island showed up on the navigation system and I had no problem in spotting the narrow unsurfaced track that led to the shore-side landing. I pulled up in a small parking area, from where a path led down to a wooden jetty. To the side of it stood a boathouse, cocooned by a mass of shrubs and trees – almost as if camouflaged. I was disappointed, but not surprised, to find the door securely locked. To the left of it hung a wooden box whose front opened with a simple latch giving access to what looked like an old-fashioned telephone. A small panel sported a button with instructions to "Press to ring". Putting the phone to my ear, I pressed the button and heard a distant burring, and waited ... and waited. I waited for perhaps half a minute but, with no reply, I returned the handset to its cradle and tried again – nothing. Either it was not functioning, or there was nobody in the house.

Peering through some wide cracks in the old wooden timbers confirmed that there was a boat inside, but I was not prepared to break down the door – even if it were possible. I wondered briefly whether I might be able to get the boat out from the water end of the building. However, since this would mean entering the water anyway, I decided to make the short swim to the island.

The water was not as cold as the last time I had entered it, and within a few minutes, I was once again climbing the concrete steps. As I rounded the house, I called out, "Anyone at home?" but there was no response. I tried the main door and, finding it locked, made my way around to the rear terrace and peered through the large glass doors.

I rocked back in amazement at the sight that greeted me. Gone was the neat and tidy room I had last seen. It appeared to have been ransacked. Broken dining chairs lay all over the floor. Papers and other debris were scattered everywhere. I could not see directly into the kitchen itself, but cooking implements littered the doorway, and items of cutlery and broken crockery covered the whole floor. What had happened here?

I rattled the doors, but these too were locked. If there had been a break-in, there must surely be some other signs of forced entry. I started to inspect the remainder of the house for broken windows but halted in my tracks almost immediately as I noticed that the previously grey stone of the patio was now stained with a strange pinkish wash. When I examined it further, I could see that at the edges of the path and in other crevices there were collections of darker, redder, sometimes almost brown substances. Linking this with the turmoil in the house, I quickly concluded that this was almost certainly blood – and lots of it. The overnight rain had diluted and dissipated it, but there was no doubt in my mind.

A sensation of dread overcame me, and I began to ponder the implications. Had Selene been hurt? Indeed, was she alive? Even then, I began to wonder whether I would ever see her again.

A new feeling – one of panic then hit me. Could the perpetrator still be on the island? Was my own life in danger perhaps? Hurriedly, I circled the house but could see no sign of a break-in. I realised I had to notify the police. I could do nothing more without them. Selene had said that there was no telephone in the house, so the nearest was my mobile in the car. As I rapidly made my way back to the landing stage, I noticed other patches of blood on the stone pathway, some darker than others. And again, on the landing, there was more blood soaked into the grain of the wood.

When I reached the car, I hurriedly dug out my mobile and dialled 112 – the number Angie had instilled into me to call in case of emergencies. A man answered impressively quickly, gabbling away equally quickly in unintelligible Italian. With no hope of understanding, I asked him if he spoke English and, after a short pause, a pleasant female voice said, "Hello. Can I help you?"

After giving her my name, I started with a very brief resume of the situation and explained that I didn't want to touch anything more until the police arrived to investigate. "There may be someone still inside the house – perhaps injured," I said breathlessly. "But I would have to smash my way in to find out ..."

"Don't do that," she broke in. "Do not touch anything until our men arrive. They will be there in about fifteen minutes. Please stay where you are. OK?"

"Yes," I agreed. I looked around. "But how do I explain where I am ..."

"We know that already, Sir," she cut in. And then, "The house you talk about is the one on the island. Yes?"

"Yes," I said, somewhat startled. "But how the hell ... oh, it doesn't matter ... I suppose you have my telephone number as well?"

"Yes, Sir. Please keep it on. If you have to telephone again, please ask for Julieta. I am assigned to this incident for the moment."

"Before you go, I need to ask about transport on the lake – boats. The one belonging to the property is locked in a shed, and I had to swim over to the island. Is there some sort of police boat on the lake?"

"I'll check, Sir. I believe so. The police are already on their way. They will know what to do."

"OK. I'll wait here then. Thanks for your help."

"Bye, Signor Ramsay. Thank you for reporting the incident."

By this time, my body was almost dry but I towelled myself down and dressed to await the arrival of the police. Several different forces make up the Italian police. Some of them are military and others civilian. Some are centrally organised as State agencies, whilst others are local. Each has its different structure and uniforms. They are co-ordinated by liaison committees but, from what I had understood, it would be something of a lottery as to which of the two principal forces would turn up.

Eventually, it was two officers of the Polizia, the ones without the posh uniforms, who arrived with impressive speed and screeched to a halt in the car park in a cloud of dust. They had brought with them a surly-looking little man who hung back as all three approached me. The two police officers could have been brothers, they shared so many similar features – swarthy, black-haired, good-looking. I have no idea whether he was of higher rank, but one of them came forward and introduced himself as Marco, and his colleague as Sergio. We all shook hands.

Turning briefly to the little man behind him, Marco continued in broken English, "Signor Francini here is locksmith. He will open the boathouse, and also house on island. We must search house and the entire island. When these are good, we will wait for Ispettore Grimaldi. He will be here in police boat – maybe one hour. No evidence to be ..." he paused, searching for the right word, "to be moved by us or by you, Signor Ramsay. Do you understand?"

"Perfectly," I agreed. "May I at least travel with you to the island? I know the place, and could be useful to you."

The two men looked at each other and then nodded, "But you not touch anything," Marco repeated.

The locksmith had already peeled away to start work on the boathouse, and in no time he had both the entrance and lakeside doors open. The boat was not large but seemed big enough for the four of us. There were a couple of oars hanging from the ceiling, but I could see no sign of any rowlocks on the gunwales. On a rack to the side lay a small outboard motor, but it would need to be mounted and I suggested that it would be simpler to use the paddles that were already lying in the boat. Marco and Sergio again looked at each other for mutual assistance and then nodded rather nervously.

I was just about to step into the boat when I spotted blood on one of the thwarts, and then more lying in the bottom of the boat. I managed to stop myself and held up my hand.

"There is blood in the boat. It could be important evidence. We cannot use it, I'm afraid."

The two police officers craned their necks to look, and it took no time for Marco to agree, "He is correct. We not use this boat." Turning to me, he announced, "We will telephone for orders," and they both marched off hurriedly towards their car.

Realising that he too would now have to wait for the Inspector, Francini was looking even grumpier than before. I walked away from him and sat on the grass under a tree looking out over the lake to the island. The discovery of blood in the boat had unsettled me still further. Strange tricks play on an anxious mind, and I was now almost convinced that Selene had been murdered, or at least badly hurt. As I waited, I could now clearly visualise the whole incident. Starting with some sort of dispute, it had quickly escalated into a frenzied attack on the fragile and helpless girl, ending with her body being dragged into the boat and dumped overboard somewhere in the middle of the lake. And Pino was the prime suspect – indeed, he was the only suspect at this moment.

Even in the beautiful setting that surrounded me, I felt utterly miserable. I had already lost my goddess.

Chapter 5

It was more like two hours before the police launch rounded the island and tied up at the jetty. Inspector Grimaldi hopped ashore and shook hands with the two police officers, whom he clearly knew. After a few words, he left them and came over to introduce himself to me. He was a narrow man. Everything about him was narrow – a slim body, a gaunt sallow face, an aquiline nose underscored by a short stubby moustache that sat precariously over a rather mean little mouth. His pale skin was made to look paler still by his jet-black hair that was slicked back, and relieved only slightly by a few strands of grey at the sides. Somehow, it was only these few signs of age that inspired any degree of confidence.

"Inspector Grimaldi," he announced in an assured and unexpectedly deep voice. "I am sorry to have kept you waiting." First appearances may be deceptive, I thought.

And at least he spoke good English. Holding a printout of the report I had made to the emergency telephone line he began, "I would like you to give me some more details – but in due course. For the moment, I think we should all go out to the island to establish the situation there. Whilst we are here, though, I would like to inspect the boat. I understand that you were unable to use it because you saw some blood in it. Is that correct?"

"Yes," I paused briefly before continuing, "At least, I think it may be blood. It's on the seats and in the bottom of the boat."

"OK. Let's go." He beckoned to the whole party to follow him. He had taken full control of the investigation.

We all trooped over to the boathouse, where a bored Francini was pacing up and down. There was no room for all of us inside, so it was just Inspector Grimaldi, Marco and myself who began the inspection. Marco had retrieved a powerful torch from the car and played it onto the suspicious areas.

"Hmm," muttered Grimaldi non-committedly. "It is possible. We will have to get Forensics to have a look."

He scratched his head silently for a few seconds and then came up with a decision.

"We will almost certainly need forensic support on the island too. Marco, please phone in and get them out here as soon as possible – on my authority. Then join us on the launch. We'll wait for you."

As Marco left, Grimaldi took the torch from him and peered closely once again at the red-stained areas of woodwork. "Hmm," he said again, and we both walked out and clambered aboard the police launch.

Within five minutes, we tied up at the island's landing. Francini, armed with a leather bag full of skeleton keys, files and other instruments, was despatched to open up the front door. The sky had darkened and rain clouds were threatening again, so it was important that we examined the suspected blood before the heavens opened and it became further diluted. We all walked around the house to the upper patio and, after a further "Hmm" or two from Grimaldi, the french doors rolled open and Francini emerged. "Tutto è aperto," he announced briefly and stepped back inside just as the rain began to spot.

"I hope Forensics arrive soon," said Grimaldi, looking up to the heavens, "before this stuff really gets going again."

With that, he dug into one of his pockets and took out a couple of small plastic phials. "It is not the correct equipment for this, but it might be better than nothing." He opened up the long blade of a Swiss army knife and began scraping at the darker patches in the joints of the paving, depositing the shavings into the jars. "That will have to do," he muttered.

Marco emerged onto the terrace and reported to Grimaldi, speaking rapidly in Italian. Grimaldi nodded acceptance, then turned to me. "My men have searched the whole house. It's in a mess, but there are no bodies, dead or alive."

I nodded and thanked him. I had not expected anything different. After all, I knew now that Selene's body lay at the bottom of the lake. Grimaldi went into the house and spent the next twenty minutes getting a clear picture of the scene in his mind, careful not to disturb anything before the arrival of the photographer and forensic experts.

With the rain now beginning to bucket down, the rest of us took refuge in the police launch. After a short while, we heard a siren and a second Polizia car skidded to a halt in the lakeside car park. Marco decided that we should send the launch over, get Sergio to take the locksmith back to town, and bring the new officers over to assist Marco in his search of the remainder of the island.

When Grimaldi had finished taking his samples, he called me into the small bedroom in which I had slept, and which had not suffered the violence of the rest of the house. He sat down on the edge of the bed and waved me to take the chair.

"I've just gone over your report again," he started. "You only ever saw two persons in the house. Is that right?"

"Yes."

"How well did you know them?"

"Hardly at all. I'd only met them that day."

"And how did you come to meet them?"

"I was swimming in the lake. The woman, Selene her name was, saw me and beckoned to me to come over." I hesitated a moment and then continued, "She was a very attractive woman," as if that was reason enough for me to take up the offer.

"Hmm. How did she seem to you? Was she relaxed?"

"Yes. She seemed very relaxed. We spent the whole afternoon talking ..." I hesitated, wondering what Grimaldi was getting at, but before he could ask another question, I continued, "By the evening we were already making plans to meet again. As I say, she was a beautiful woman," I shrugged before adding, "I have to admit it – I was very attracted to her."

"That's alright, Sir. I get the picture. And did you get to see her again?"

"No. As I reported when I called, I tried to telephone her a number of times, but couldn't get through. The line was still dead this morning, and I didn't like the thought of never seeing her again, so I came over. That's when I saw all this mess and called 112."

"I'm not surprised you couldn't get through on the phone, Sir. I found a smashed mobile in the kitchen. I'll bet good money that it's hers."

"Oh my God," I cursed. "That's it then. I'll not see her again, will I? What do you think happened to her?"

"That's what I'm here to find out, Sir."

"Now," Grimaldi continued. "If you were interested in her, I assume that the man isn't her husband or boyfriend?"

I laughed. "No," I said, but then hesitated before repeating, "No. At least, I'm almost sure he isn't. He's Italian certainly – she called him Pino. I got the impression he was some sort of hired help, maybe with medical or nursing training. Selene is handicapped – she is paralysed from the waist down. He pushed her around in a wheelchair."

"Oh." The Inspector looked surprised. "I didn't know that. It wasn't in your report."

"No," I admitted, rather defensively. "Probably not – it was only brief."

"That's fine, Sir. So – was he local?"

"I'm guessing so. I don't know for certain."

"But he wasn't a relative of any sort?"

"Not as far as I know. Again, I'm guessing. There were no obvious signs of affection between them. It seemed to be a strictly professional relationship."

"Did she mention his second name?"

"No. I don't think so. She referred to him as 'my man', I remember. Otherwise, it was just Pino."

"Did you notice any animosity – any friction between them?"

I thought for a second or two. "He seemed a bit grumpy in the morning, but no – not really. It generally seemed to be a cool, mistress and servant relationship."

Grimaldi silently made a few notes in a black flip-over notebook. Then he stared into faraway space for a short while before continuing, "But you saw him clearly. You could pick him out if we showed you some photographs?"

"Yes. Definitely."

After another pause for thought and a suck on the end of his ballpoint, "Now ... did your conversations with Selene give you any clues as to her identity – her second name perhaps, or where she lives?"

Again, I had to think about this. "I don't think so. It seems she was ..." I stopped myself. I couldn't bear to write her off yet. "... It seems she *is* some sort of socialite. She moves around the world attending all the big sporting and social events. I don't know if she is rich herself, or whether she has wealthy and powerful friends, but she seems to move in those sorts of circles."

"But she is English?"

"Yes. Although she said her mother was Greek."

The Inspector was again sucking his pen and looking vacantly towards the heavens.

"OK," he said suddenly. "That'll do for now I think. But you will have to make a full written statement. And I will need to speak to you again. Where can I get hold of you, please?"

I gave him the address of our cottage and my mobile number. "Would you like my address in England too," I asked. "I'll be returning there in a few days."

"Hmm." The Inspector thought for a moment. "That may not be a good idea. If this does turn out to be blood, it might well become a case of murder – and you will be a principal witness. We'll have to think about that."

Principal witness, I thought, and then suddenly realised that I would probably also be the principal suspect.

As Grimaldi was saying this, Marco knocked briefly and entered the room. Speaking in Italian, he told the Inspector that the forensic team had arrived and that he had sent the launch over for them.

"Good. Thank you," Grimaldi acknowledged.

When Marco had left, the Inspector remained seated on the edge of the bed, tapping his notebook idly with the ballpoint. "Right. I expect you'll want to get off now. Unfortunately, we're a bit stuck for water transport. I'll get the launch to take you ashore as soon as the forensics team is installed."

"Thanks, Inspector."

"Now, I want your report as soon as possible – it's better made soon after the incident. I could get you to come all the way over to my office." He smiled, and then continued, "But would you prefer to write it in your own time – well, tonight preferably? Do you have access to a computer?"

"Yes, I do – but I don't have a printer," and as an afterthought, "I could put it on a stick, or I could email it to you."

"Hmm. I usually have a memory stick on me. I'll make sure I have one tomorrow." After a brief pause, he continued, "Because I'd like to meet you in the morning – just to complete the picture. I want to see your house and the place where you started your swim the other day. I'll be on the same launch tomorrow. How will I find you?"

I thought for a moment, and then said, "Come to the village. There's only one – just around the bend on the opposite shore. It has a small jetty where you can tie up, and I'll meet you there and drive you around to whatever you want to see. What time will you be there?"

"That sounds good. Nine o'clock OK?"

"Fine. I'll be there."

By this time, we could hear the noise of the new arrivals, and Grimaldi went out to greet them. He broke away briefly and spoke to the launch driver, who immediately beckoned to me to follow him.

Arriving back on the mainland, I was passing the boathouse door when I spotted a faded sign, which I had not noticed earlier. Looking more closely, it turned out to be a rather classy brass plate, but it had weathered badly over the years and now merged into the wooden background. The engraved writing was still clearly legible, however. At the top was written "The House in the Lake" – unimaginative perhaps, but certainly descriptive. Underneath it read "For all enquiries", followed by a telephone number beginning 0044 – an English number, of which I made a careful note.

It seems that the world over, any police car arriving at a crime scene will screech to a halt and be abandoned pointing in any random direction. In the lake's small parking area, five police vehicles had now arrived in this untidy manner, and it took me some time to manoeuvre my way out. But once on the road, I was back in our village within twenty minutes. By now, it was early evening and I stopped off at the bar for a couple of beers and a bite to eat. A small group of locals were drinking and spitting words at each other like machine guns, as only Italians can. I felt very much alone and sat quietly in a corner with my Carbonara.

It had been a long day and the adrenaline generated by the events of the afternoon was dissipating fast. This left me with thoughts of Selene's brutal murder, and nursing the void of my own loss. Maybe it was the thought of such vicious treatment being visited on this vulnerable creature, but I suddenly realised then how infatuated I had become. And now she was gone.

I spent the evening typing my report, detailing all my recollections from the time I first entered the lake up to the time I emerged from it on the following day.

The Inspector arrived precisely on time and I drove him up to the house. We copied my report onto his memory stick and over a cup of coffee, he showed polite interest in my plans for the place. He told me that he had heard nothing from the forensic team and it would be several days before they completed their various tests. Back down in the village, I left him pottering around the recreation area, which was located only about a hundred metres from the jetty and his boat.

I threw myself into work over the next few days, in the hope that it would help disperse some of the heavy clouds that had gathered in my mind. It was partly successful, but I was now also feeling a degree of guilt over my infidelity to Angie, albeit platonic. I decided to appease these thoughts by completing the shower room – something that I knew would please her.

I did meet with Inspector Grimaldi one last time before I left for England. I was putting the final touches to the shower room when he telephoned. There was not much news, he reported, but he would be happy to meet me the following morning when he would be overseeing the final day of investigations on the site.

The car park was almost full when I arrived, but I immediately spotted the Inspector who was on the jetty, deep in discussion with a couple of men in frogmen gear. As I walked towards him, he broke off and moved to greet me.

"Good morning, Signor Ramsay. How are you?"

"Well thanks," I assured him. "It's good of you to see me."

"Well, we'll be winding up the investigation today, and I wanted to show that we haven't been idle." With that, he gently cupped my elbow and eased me in the direction of the jetty. "We'll go over to the house and I'll fill you in on our progress."

As we boarded the police launch, the two frogmen were diving into the muddy waters of the lake. Impressive, I thought. I had not expected that.

I was further surprised as we entered the house, for it had been restored to the state it was in when I had first seen it. Grimaldi must have noticed my reaction and said, "We released the house yesterday from being an official crime scene. The owners arranged for a team to come in to clean it up. It's a great little place, isn't it?"

"Yes," I agreed, "I have good memories of it." I meant of Selene, of course, and the Inspector knew it.

"I understand," he said. "Look. There's no need to think that something serious has happened to her. There's no real evidence for it at all. The blood analysis is very inconclusive, I'm afraid. All the overnight rain had both diluted and contaminated it. I don't know if you know, but DNA can only be obtained from the white cells in blood – red cells have no nuclei, and therefore no DNA. The experts tell me there is no chance of getting firm evidential quality DNA of any individual – there's not even a clear-cut case for the sex. It could even be animal blood. I believe you said she had a dog." He paused for a moment before continuing, "And there wasn't as much blood as you might have thought. The rain had spread it very thinly." Again, he paused for a moment or two, planning how to continue.

"I have to be honest, Sir, with no clear evidence of any serious crime, we simply cannot justify spending any more time on this investigation. Like everywhere else in the world, our police agencies are under ever-increasing financial pressure. On the other hand, we don't want you to go bleating to the British press about Italian police work. We had quite enough of that following the Amanda Knox case. Don't get me wrong. I'm sure mistakes were made, but we were stung by the amount of uninformed comments and criticism."

"So I've got some divers out today. They'll trawl the lake bottom between the island and the shore. I think you'll agree that we can't hope to check the whole lake. And then that's it, I'm afraid – at least until a body or some such new evidence comes to light. I'm sorry."

I didn't have to think about it too long. I could see their problem. "I understand," I assured him. "Have you got anywhere with identifying the house's occupants?"

"No. It's still a mystery. Your people have made enquiries to the owner's agents, but they didn't seem to get anywhere. With the investigation now over, I don't propose to spend any more time on it."

"OK, Inspector," I said. "I'll be going back to England tomorrow. You have my address and telephone number if you need me. And if you do find anything more, perhaps you would be good enough to let me know."

"Certainly," agreed Grimaldi. He dug out his police warrant and handed me a card. "Give me a ring if you hear anything new. Now, if you've seen all you want here I'll take you back to your car."

And that seemed to be the end of my little adventure. I tidied up the house, leaving the new bathroom in sparkling condition, waiting for Angie to admire it on her next visit.

I set off at the crack of dawn the following day, but it's a long drive home and I always take a couple of days, staying overnight somewhere on a choice of farms around the Orleans area. Angie seemed pleased to see me when I got in the following day. She had prepared an excellent welcome home dinner, and I went to bed happy enough that the curtain had come down, and that life had returned to normal.

It could not last, of course.

Chapter 6

Two or three days passed without incident, and I was able to get the rest I needed. Angie seemed more content than I had known her recently, which I put down to the return of the wanderer. We slept together in our large double bed, but she made no overtures for any sexual contact and I was very happy to let it pass.

With Angie at work each day, I tried to busy myself with some of the household chores – something that doesn't come naturally to me. But without the structure of a job, I had time on my hands, which I felt no inclination to fill by taking up golf or any other leisure pastime. My thoughts turned to the future of our Italian house, and I started to plan my next trip.

It was a Wednesday, I recall. I have good reason to remember it now, but I signally failed to do so at the time. For Wednesdays are the day that rubbish is collected, and as she left for work that morning, Angie had even reminded me to put out the bins. Also, would I please collect some dry cleaning, as she needed a particular skirt for that evening?

I had normally priced my larger property developments using professionally produced bills of quantities, but I had prepared numerous estimates for smaller projects using rudimentary schedules of the work involved. I was very conscious that I had entirely neglected to plan our Italian job with any such detail. It was very much "seat of the pants" stuff because I had not considered formal estimates to be necessary. I knew that I had sufficient funds and that it would simply cost whatever it cost. But now I decided that I really should prepare something, and after I had cleared away breakfast, got out the plans I had drawn up for the Italian Planners and set to work on my computer. It requires both time and concentration, and I was soon lost to the world.

I did break a couple of times, for coffee and a sandwich, but otherwise kept going throughout the day, only stopping with a jolt as I heard the front door open and Angie storm in with, "The rubbish bins are still full. Haven't they been? Don't tell me you forgot to put them out?"

Worse was to follow, of course. She had returned home early because we were due to meet friends for dinner, and she immediately demanded to know whether the outfit she had planned for the occasion was still at the dry cleaners. I was duly apologetic, but there was to be no pacifying her. The period of calm was over, and she refused to let it go – embarrassingly, even in front of our friends.

Looking back now, I believe it was this unremarkable little tiff that signalled the demise of our marriage. We must both have been aware of the problems, but we had ignored them for far too long, and

I doubted whether counselling would be of any help at this stage. We had to talk. But not right now.

And so it was that Selene came back into my thoughts. I had been surprised by how easily I had let her go following my parting meeting with Inspector Grimaldi. I would be lying if I claimed I had not thought of her at all. In quiet moments, day or night, brief memories had returned, like my first glimpse of her legs – works of art, but now known to be useless.

But now my thoughts became more constructive. They were no longer the idle erotic fantasies I had experienced after our first meeting. This was now a damsel in distress. I had no idea how badly she was hurt, or even if she was alive at all, but over time I became convinced that she needed my help. The Italian police authorities had washed their hands of the mystery, and I could well be her sole champion. One way or another, I had to discover what had happened that day at the House in the Lake.

I was serious about it now and opened a file boldly marked SELENE. First into the file was a printout of my statement to the Italian police. As I slipped it into the folder, I wondered what Angie would make of it all if she came across it. I had decided on the long journey home that I would not tell her of my meeting Selene. If our marriage was to break up, I had no wish to hand her ammunition for any Court proceedings. And once I had made that decision, it was much too late to break it to her now.

There was little else for the file. I stapled Inspector Grimaldi's card to the front cover and sat back to consider where I should start. Did I have any information that the Italian police did not have? One area that I felt they had not addressed very thoroughly was the identities of Selene and Pino. If I could just find out Selene's surname...

It hit me like an electric shock – I recall actually jumping in my seat – Selene's mobile phone! Grimaldi had said that they had come across it in the chaos of the house. It would surely hold the names and telephone numbers of her friends. They would be able to give me any amount of information. Excited now, I reached for the phone and dialled the number on Grimaldi's card. After only a few seconds, I was greeted by a stream of Italian. Summoning up my best accent, I asked for "Ispettore Grimaldi, per favore." Silence and a couple of clicks later I heard his voice, "Pronto".

"Hello Inspector," I opened. "It's Martin Ramsay here. You remember me – the house in Lake Tousle?"

"Yes, Signor Ramsay. What can I do for you?"

"I assume there have been no developments in the case?"

"No. Nothing. As I told you, the file is closed."

"I was just thinking about the girl's identity, Inspector. You said that you had found Selene's mobile phone. Did you have it examined? Did her phonebook have details of her contacts?"

"Signor Ramsay, I am a policeman – this is not a dating agency." He went quiet then, as did I – feeling somewhat sheepish.

"But I'll tell you," he continued finally. "I should perhaps have told you at our last meeting. It turned out not to be her phone, I'm afraid. The SIM card was intact and we ran it through the technical labs. The contacts list merely consisted of local emergency and other useful services. The last call was to a local dentist, but that was more than six months earlier. It seems that the house's owners had provided it for the benefit of the occupants. I'm sorry, we got no useful information."

"Oh," I said sadly, very disappointed. "That's a pity. Well, I'm sorry I disturbed you, Inspector." We said our goodbyes and once again promised to keep in touch should anything new occur.

The news upset me. To have such a promising idea dashed so swiftly was not easy to take, and I remember wondering whether my quest was already dead in the water.

That night, I pondered other ways to discover her identity. And Pino – it seemed that his identity was equally obscure.

Suddenly, I recalled Selene remarking that someone – I think she referred to him as her agent – had booked the house for her here in England. How could I find this person? Grimaldi might know, but it was too soon to telephone him again. He had clearly not appreciated my call, and I could not afford to alienate him completely.

It was not until early morning that it suddenly struck me. The plaque on the side of the boathouse – I remembered jotting down a contact telephone number for the owner. He would surely know the name of the person who had booked it for her. But where had I written it? I always keep a small notebook in the car's glove compartment, essentially to make notes in the case of an accident. It was too early to go out to the car, but the longer I lay there, the more convinced I became that I would find the number there.

I managed to contain my eagerness until after breakfast and Angie had left for work. I was prepared to be disappointed once again, but there it was on the second page of the notebook – no name, just a telephone number. I grabbed the phone and punched in the number. Thankfully, it began to ring.

And it continued to ring. "Damn," I muttered under my breath. I looked up at the clock. If the number was for an office, it may be too early. If it was an individual, maybe they had already left for work. I tried the number again at various times that day, but always with the same lack of response. Frustrated, towards the end of the afternoon, I googled the number and was delighted to get a result. Even though I am well versed in computers, the speed and extent of results from Google searches never cease to amaze me. The information it produced that day was not much, but it did add a name to my embryo database – "Home and Away", described as an agency for "the letting of properties all over England and across Europe". There was even a small map showing its location on the edge of Wadhurst, a small Sussex village. There were no names or further details, but it was a start and gave me a lift.

At that very moment, Angie came in and I hurriedly tucked the file away amongst the schedules of building work.

As soon as she left for work the following day, I rang the number again but got no response. By lunchtime, there was still no reply and I began to wonder whether the firm existed at all. But gradually, fresh plans were forming in my mind that would govern my activities for the next several weeks. I found that I was enjoying this detective work. It had been frustrating so far, but it created a welcome challenge for me. I had both the time and the motivation, and it fed into my fantasies. I had not given up the notion that I might find Selene alive, and win her over. I would become her champion – her knight in shining armour.

The following day ushered in the weekend, and Angie and I would be together for a couple of edgy days. She had arranged to meet some friends from work and left the house late on Saturday afternoon, leaving me to plan my moves for the coming week, and I was already asleep before she returned.

The telephone remained unanswered on Monday, and I plotted a route to Wadhurst. I knew it was south of the river, which is alien territory for me, and I guessed it would take at least a couple of hours. With several things to do around the house, it was nearly midday before I left.

A sorry sight greeted my eyes when I finally stood in front of Home and Away. Tucked towards the end of a cul-de-sac, it appeared to be a type of shop but was very decrepit. The paintwork was old, faded and peeling, with the window glass cracked and dirty. The only redeeming feature was the entrance door – it was open, offering hope that someone was present.

The state of the exterior had accurately foreshadowed the sad scene that awaited me as I pressed on through the doorway. I guessed it had probably once been some sort of travel agency, and most of its fittings had been re-used. It was sparsely furnished with a couple of spindly chairs facing an old counter, which was now entirely bare. Affixed to the wall behind the counter were the only signs of any form of commercial activity – some postcard-sized photographs of residential properties of all quality and sizes.

No human presence was either visible or audible as I waited, wondering how to proceed in such a strange environment. After a moment or two, I shouted out, "Hello. Is anybody there?"

After a short pause and the noise of a chair scraping the floor came an answer, "I'll be with you in a second." A door behind the counter shortly opened wide and was immediately filled by the figure of a woman. To say she was large would be an understatement. She was enormous. Two tree trunks for legs supported hips that reached from jamb to jamb, with an upper body to match. Any initial reaction was soon supplanted by one of sympathy for the disabling consequences of such a size – the restrictions on movement, the looks from strangers and the likely difficulty in making friends.

If there was anything to lift the gloomy picture, it was her face. Although certainly chubby and highly coloured, it was blessed with fine features and a welcoming smile on its lips that announced, "Hi. I'm Sharon."

I hesitated briefly as my review of her ended with the hair that topped this oddly pretty face. A straggly, unkempt light brown mess sadly suggested the loss of any interest in fighting a losing battle with her appearance.

"Hi," I managed eventually. "My name's Martin – Martin Ramsay."

"Do come through," she said. Backing away from the door, she turned and waddled off into her office. I followed her but, having to skirt around the counter, arrived only in time to see her slump heavily down into a large chair behind an old utilitarian desk. In front of it were two high-backed chairs and she indicated one to me as she settled back. I briefly took in the rest of the room, which was as sparingly furnished as the outer office. A bank of four filing cabinets occupied one wall, whilst another housed a simple table holding a printer. In one corner, a coat stand stood bare except for one battered umbrella. On her desk were a couple of files, one of them open, along with a notepad and a small collection of ballpoints and pencils. A computer lay in front of her, but its green monochrome monitor suggested that it was probably not born in this century.

"What can I do for you, Martin?" she asked, with another of her winning smiles.

"I've been trying to get hold of you on the telephone ..." I began.

"I'm sorry," she cut in immediately. "I'm on my own now, and nearly all my work is done online nowadays. I do try to get into the office on most days, but it's usually only for a short time. I really ought to get this telephone number linked to my home. I've mentioned it to my boss, but he won't do anything about it."

"That's not very good for business."

"That's what I tell him. But turnover's not good, and he doesn't want to spend the money."

"Oh well, it's meant that I've had quite a long journey here. I do hope you'll be able to help me," I began, in the hope that sympathy might oil the wheels to a result. "I wanted to ask about a property in Italy."

"Ah," she broke in. "The House in the Lake. We've only got the one in Italy."

As she was speaking, she tapped into the computer, presumably calling up the property's details onto her screen. "How did you learn of it?" she asked.

"I've been there," I replied. "I was there a couple of weeks ago."

This seemed to interest her and she leant forward. "You were?" she exclaimed. "There was some sort of problem there – a break-in or a fight of some sort. We had a policeman round, asking questions. I couldn't help him though …"

"I know about it. I was there. It was me that called in the local Italian police."

"What happened?" she asked earnestly.

"Nobody knows," I replied. "When I got there, the whole place had been ransacked, and there was blood on the terrace, but nobody around. The police carried out some investigations but couldn't get anything from the blood. With no body, and with no one reported missing, they had no option but to close the case."

"How very odd. We were simply advised to get the place cleaned up."

"Anyway," I began, without really thinking how I was going to pursue the subject. "I'm not entirely happy with the way it's been left. I was wondering if you could let me know who made the last booking for the house."

"Oh, I'm sorry," she said immediately. "That's confidential information. I can't tell you that. I wouldn't even tell the police. I referred them to the owner – left it up to him to decide. I'm sorry."

That was a blow, but I had half expected it. "I don't want to get anyone into trouble," I started. "I won't pass it on to the police – here, or in Italy. It's a personal thing. Someone I met there. I want to get in touch with her."

This seemed to trigger a spark of interest in her, and I continued quickly, "To tell you the truth, I rather fell for this lady. I liked her a lot. She told me that someone over here had arranged the booking for her."

Sharon hesitated, and again I continued rapidly. "Please. I've driven a long way today. I want to find her."

She hesitated once again, and I held my breath. Then, after a second or two, she very suddenly coughed, and then again. After that, she could not stop, but said between coughs, "I'm sorry" and, "I'll just go and get some water." With that, she struggled out of her chair, covering her mouth, and lurched towards the door. As she did so, she brushed against the monitor, knocking it around so that it pointed in my direction. It was clumsy, but it was also a clear invitation for me to take the information I wanted from the screen.

As soon as she disappeared, I reached for her notepad and a pencil and tilted the screen around further toward me. Looking down the entries, there had only been a couple this year – the last on the 21st of May. This was the one I was after, and I scribbled down the address and telephone number of a certain Robertson Courtney, ripped off the page and stuffed it into my back pocket.

Placing the pad and pencil back where I had found them, I considered whether I should return the screen to face Sharon, but before I could do so, she came back in apologising once again for her coughing fit.

She sat down, adjusting the screen and saying, "I'm so sorry I can't help you, Mr Ramsay. I do hope you understand my position."

"Yes, perfectly," I said. "Thank you for seeing me anyway."

"Well. I hope you find your lady somehow."

There was nothing more to say then. "Don't get up, Sharon. I can find my way out." She smiled as I left her, and I remember hoping that she had perhaps gained something from her helping hand.

I strode out into the warm afternoon sunshine with a lighter step. I was getting somewhere at last. I am not normally given to riding my luck, and my initial reaction was to head home and consolidate the news into a new plan of action. However, the nature of

Sharon's agency led me to believe that their client was likely to be a local man, and it would save time and petrol if I were able to see him that same afternoon. I sat in the car with the door open and dialled the number for Mr Courtney. It rang for some time, and I began to expect an automatic answering system to cut in. This gave me a moment of panic as I hadn't given any consideration to my approach. What message could I leave? But just as I had decided to hang up, I heard "Hello" in an educated male voice.

"Robertson Courtney?" I asked.

There was a moment's silence before the voice continued, "Who is asking, please."

"My name is Martin Ramsay. You don't know me, but we have a mutual friend. I'd like a brief word with you about her if that's possible please."

"I'm sorry, Mr Courtney is not here."

"Oh. That's a pity," I said. After a moment's thought I continued, "I'm only in the area for the day. How close are you to Wadhurst by the way?"

"Not far," was the terse reply.

"Will he be back today then?"

"No. I'm afraid not."

"Oh," I said, a bit stumped. Without thinking, almost automatically, I continued, "I wonder if you'd ask him to give me a ring sometime – when he's got a moment?"

"Yes, I'll give him that message. What is your number?" I repeated my name and gave him both my home and mobile numbers, thanked him and said goodbye. As soon as I had rung off, I began to regret asking him to call. If he never phoned, it would reduce my options for telephoning again. How long should I wait for the call? I was feeling impatient now. And if he called when I was out, what would Angie make of it?

With nothing more to achieve, I drove home and was back just before Angie returned from work.

Chapter 7

Just as luck in my quest had begun to turn, so my marriage was about to take a dive into more perilous, even terminal, depths.

The evening started well enough, with Angie even giving me a short peck of a kiss as she passed by me in the entrance hall. Before she had left for work that morning, we agreed on pork chops for supper, and I had picked up a pack on my way back from Sussex. As had become our custom, I had laid out the main ingredients neatly on the worktop, along with some potatoes I had peeled and a salad ready to be dressed. The rest was down to Angie – neither of us was willing to trust any further action by me.

On most days, we managed to polish off a bottle of wine over our evening meal and we were well over half way through one of our favourite whites, when Angie asked where I had been today. Failing to spot the deliberate trap, I made some vague references to the difficulties I was having with the Italian building schedule and implied that I had spent most of the day on it.

"Something's wrong with our phone then," she said immediately. "I've been trying to get hold of you most of the day."

I was wrong-footed and flustered. She never normally phoned during the day, and no immediate response came to mind. I managed to buy some time with, "What did you want me for, darling?"

"Never mind that," she retorted, obviously annoyed. "It wasn't very important, but where were you?"

"I told you. I was here, working on my figures. I get involved, and I don't always answer the phone ..."

"Liar," she broke in loudly. "You always answer the phone. You can't bear the thought of someone missing you."

"And I had to go out shopping for dinner," I added, an opportune afterthought coming to mind.

"Rubbish," she exclaimed. "That wouldn't take more than an hour. You were gone most of the day. Where were you, for God's sake?"

"I've told you," I insisted, but rather unconvincingly.

"Have you found yourself a lover?" she accused, her voice raised in anger now.

"No," I was able to assure her truthfully, and then with a matching degree of indignant anger. "Don't you think you'd know if I had?"

"Well you haven't noticed," she came back immediately – too quickly, unthinking.

The world around us went silent then. I tried to think whether I had heard her correctly and, if I had, could I have perhaps misunderstood. Was there any other interpretation I could put on her remark?

And for her part, Angie was visibly shaken by her sudden disclosure. It had slipped out – like a fumbled slip catch and, like that, was now irretrievable. The damage was done, and there was no going back. As this dawned, she began to see the admission in a new light. It was now in the open – something she had always known would happen someday but, for a variety of reasons, she had put off for nearly two years.

The few seconds of silence seemed like minutes. It was Angie who finally ended them with, "I'm sorry, Martin. I didn't mean it to come out like that."

I said nothing for a moment or two. "You'd better tell me about it," I said quietly. We had finished our meal and I filled our glasses. "Let's go next door. Bring your drink."

Once we had settled, I waited, expecting her to start explaining her remark. When she remained silent, I opened with, "Who is he? Do I know him?"

"Yes," she said simply, and then added, "Simon."

Simon Brotherton was her high-flying boss. I had met him on several occasions and rather liked him. Urbane, charming and no doubt very clever, he was nevertheless no great looker and I had never perceived him as a threat.

"*Simon Brotherton?*" I queried, perhaps sounding rather too surprised.

"He's a good man," she countered defensively. I could see that tears were beginning to form in her eyes now. Was this remorse? I was prepared to accept that. My mind was only now slowly beginning to form a clear reaction to the news. The immediate anger caused by the betrayal was gradually becoming superseded by other emotions – surprise that Angie had been the adulterer; it could so easily have been me. But more and more, I began to feel a degree of comfort, almost of relief that the sad state of our marriage was finally out in the open, and that some form of resolution was now in sight.

"Tell me about it," I said firmly, but gently.

She had been living the lie for almost two years and the whole story poured out in a structured torrent which suggested that, whilst perhaps not exactly rehearsed, she had often run the sequence though her mind for just such a moment.

Their work had thrown them together. On business trips, they had frequently found themselves alone together for meals in restaurants, drinks in bars, and preparing for meetings in hotel rooms. They had found much in common – in theatre, literature, music and eventually in the states of their respective marriages. The inevitable happened after only a short time, and they found considerable harmony too in their lovemaking. The relationship had strengthened and intensified with many of the foreign business trips being devoid of any meaningful business. He had two children, twin girls, who he quite naturally adored, and for the first eighteen months or so, they had both been content to let their liaison bumble along in secret. More recently, however, with increasing disaffection in her marriage, Angie had felt a greater desire to formalise their relationship and had made overtures to him.

"You tell me you think Denise is becoming suspicious, Simon," she had begun. "The girls are teenagers now, and they're going to be getting ideas of their own soon. We must start thinking of our future. I hope that's what you want – a future together." But nothing had yet been resolved.

I listened quietly until she finished with a final, "I'm sorry, Martin. It just happened."

After a considerable pause, I said, "I can't say that the change in our relationship has gone unnoticed, but I didn't expect that. I should have got us to talk earlier." Then, after a pause, I asked, "Where do we go from here, Angie?"

She didn't reply – merely shrugged, but I could see that she was close to tears once again. I went over and gave her a small but reassuring hug, to which she responded by putting her hand on my arm.

"Not now then," I said. She agreed and, with a squeeze of my arm, she got up and left the room. It had been an oddly civilised half hour, not in the least bit as I had ever imagined it would be. I felt almost guilty that I had not reacted more angrily, or put up some sort of fight to keep her. But I felt sure that we had both concluded that the marriage was unlikely to last much longer and, for our different reasons, were relieved that it was now out in the open.

I felt shaky and needed some air and time to think. As I left the room, I just kept going and went out of the front door. I had been walking for around five minutes when I suddenly realised I was on autopilot, and had arrived at the doors of our local pub. It was one of its busier nights, but I was relieved to see no one I knew and carried my pint over to a table in a quiet corner.

It was clear that the marriage had finally breathed its last few gasps. They had been remarkably painless, and I could only hope that the final rites would turn out to be equally uncomplicated. Having no children helped greatly, as did the fact that Angie had a decent job. The house was mortgaged, but not to a great degree and I could afford to pay it off with considerable funds to spare. The house in Italy might be a problem, but it was my project in the main, and I did not believe that Angie would want any continuing interest.

Suddenly, I faced a cluster of new tasks that would eat into my time and money. Lawyers would need to be instructed, investments sold, property divided, and one or other of us would have to find a new place to live. All this, and more, would detract from the renovation work on the Italian property ... and the hunt for Selene.

Ah! Selene. I suddenly realised that I was free for her. I could give my fantasies full rein. Rarely would an hour pass, day or night, without an image of her passing idly across my mind. Mostly, they were happy pictures, as I had known her that day – laughing and full of life. But in the more sombre moments, I saw her face in close-up, white and cold with her lovely blue eyes, now merely empty sockets, gazing up vacantly from the depths of the lake. Was she alive or dead? I simply had to find out. I left the pub after just one beer, energized and eager to get on with the new life that lay in front of me.

When I got home, Angie was waiting in the living room, finishing off the bottle of wine. She gave me a wan smile and said, "I've made up a bed in the spare room. I'll sleep in there tonight." The wine and beer were beginning to have their effect but, if she wanted to talk, I decided I should boost them with some grain. I poured myself a whiskey, adding only the slightest splash of water.

"I've given it a lot of thought, Martin," she started. "Not just now, but over quite a long time. I knew this moment would come one day. I feel bad, and I've said how sorry I am, but I think we probably both expected it sometime. We've been drifting apart for some time. Isn't that right?"

I said nothing, and indicated no agreement, just waited for her to continue.

"Anyway, that's how I see it. Somehow, though, we have to split up the family assets. I don't intend to ask for too much, but we've achieved enough together for us both to live comfortably. I have no idea when, or even if,

Simon will ever leave his wife, so I have to be capable of living on my own – for a while at least. I have a decent job, so if you're prepared to let me have the house, free of mortgage, and money to run it, you can have the rest. I've never known the details of your investments and other assets, and I don't want to know now. Just make me an offer. If I think it's reasonable, we needn't make this too complicated or costly. As quick and inexpensive as possible – a neat split, eh?"

It sounded good to me, but I was not prepared to jump at it. I had heard too many stories of the way positions can change during divorce proceedings. "OK, Angie," I replied. "I have only ballpark figures in my head. I may have to speak to the accountants. I'll have to repay the mortgage on the house – and that may involve a fat fee. Then there'll be all the lawyers' fees and Court expenses." I thought for a moment or two but could come to no firm decision. "I'll give you a figure tomorrow night. Is that OK?"

"Fine," she agreed. "I just want us to be civilized about this, Martin."

"Suit's me," I agreed, as I downed the rest of my whiskey. She got up, and we departed to our separate bedrooms.

After breakfast, I called my friend Alastair Trimble, a solicitor I had used on many occasions over the years for contracts and conveyancing work. He knew both of us and was naturally both surprised and saddened by my news. His expertise did not lie in matrimonial cases, but he arranged a meeting for us the following day with one of his partners, Melanie Fairchild.

I had not been entirely honest about our finances on the previous evening. My type of work involves keeping in mind all manner of building costs and property values, and I always had a pretty accurate idea of our total wealth. From there, it was a quick and simple exercise to calculate a fair figure for Angie. She seemed to be prepared to settle for any reasonable sum and I certainly had no desire to short-change her. I arrived at a figure that just touched six figures, and was reasonably sure that she would find it acceptable.

With this settled, my mind was clear for Selene to take occupation of it. The majority of my friends are either married or in long-term relationships. They generally seem happy enough with their various partners, but I have noticed no evidence of the same single-minded devotion that I felt for Selene. The average person's dictionary is generally thought to consist of some 20,000 or so words, of which only a small portion is ever used in normal conversation. Some rarely used words seem strange, betraying little of their meaning or roots. "Besotted" is such a word. It had lain dormant in my vocabulary all my life, but it seemed right for me then. I was besotted with Selene. I needed to find her and be with her. I simply had to discover what had happened out there – and the trail was fast drying up.

I decided to telephone her agent again, but the same cultured voice answered.

"Robertson Courtney?" I began.

"He's not here. Who is calling?"

"It's Martin Ramsay," I said. "I called the other day and left a message for him to phone me. He hasn't done so, and it's becoming urgent now. When will he be in please?"

"He is not here, and I have no idea when he will be. I gave him your message. It is really up to him to telephone if he so wishes. I'm sorry. I can't help you."

"Is it possible ..." I started but heard a click as the receiver at the other end was replaced.

That was it. I had hit another dead end. But I knew immediately that I would not be able to leave it like that, and determined to pay a visit to Five Oaks Manor – the home of the mysterious Robertson Courtney.

Chapter 8

Melanie Fairchild failed most miserably to live up to the promise of her attractive name. Thin, wispy hair struggled to frame a pudgy face that bore all the wrinkles and defects accumulated over her sixty or so years. An archetypal feminist, I concluded, as Angie and I introduced ourselves. She could mean trouble.

But in the event, it all seemed straightforward enough. A conflict of interests meant that she could not act for both parties but, on her advice, we agreed on a compromise. She would act for Angie, whose admitted adultery would provide the necessary reason for the breakdown. She would complete all the paperwork, which would make it easy enough for me to act on my behalf. Although we had already agreed on the financial arrangements, the Court would need to check that they were reasonable, and I promised to supply all necessary details. She would put the process in train and told us that it was likely to take between three and six months. All three of us shook hands and went our separate ways.

After breakfast the following day, I left for Sussex once again. I had googled the address and downloaded a map, but it was the best part of a couple of hours before I pulled into an imposing gravel drive between stone lions lying on sturdy brick pillars. Large oak trees lined the entire length until it opened out in front of a sprawling and equally imposing house. Whoever Mr Courtney was, I knew now that he was not a poor man.

A fork in the drive branched away to a garage block at the rear, but I drove straight on and parked in front of the house. A wide porch sheltered the main entrance. As I approached the door, its ancient wooden timbers, set with black iron studs, bore testament to the age of the building. Missing from it was the chunky wrought-iron knocker that it deserved, and nor could I see any bell push. The owner seemed to be as unapproachable at home as he had been over the telephone. But eventually, I spotted a decorative iron handle sprouting from the wall some distance from the door itself. After a moment's examination, I yanked it towards me. The disappointing sound of an electronic chime from within painted a few more brush strokes to my mental picture of the elusive owner.

I waited, but could hear no movement inside. I was just about to reach for the bell again when the door opened and a young man stepped forward into the porch. Even before he opened his mouth, I knew that this was the man who had answered my telephone calls. His looks matched his voice very precisely. He was a tall thin man, good-looking in an angular sort of way. Mousy dark brown hair sprouted from his head untidily, making it look as if he had just got out of bed to answer the door. He was about my age, maybe even a trifle younger, and greeted me with the slightest trace of a smile of welcome. "Good morning. Can I be of help?"

"I'm trying to find Robertson Courtney. I believe this is his house."

"I'm afraid he's not in," he answered warily. "Are you the chap who's been telephoning for him?"

"Yes. That would be me. Martin Ramsay. I've called a couple of times and spoken to you, but each time he's been out."

"I fear you may have misunderstood me, Mr Ramsay," he said firmly. "When I said that he's not in, I perhaps should have said that he doesn't reside here – not permanently anyway."

"But it is listed as his house – surely? Do you rent it, or perhaps you're a relative?"

"I don't see that it's any of your business," he said somewhat testily.

"I'm so sorry," I cut in quickly. "I didn't mean to be rude. But I'm so frustrated. I do need to speak with Mr Courtney rather urgently now. I've driven for two hours. Is there any way I can contact him please?"

He went quiet, and I thought I might have blown forever my last remaining lead. We stood silently looking at each other for several seconds before a slight smile began playing on his lips.

"Justin," he said suddenly and offered me his hand. "I suppose I'm something between Mr Courtney's secretary, butler, and housekeeper ..." As he was saying this, I caught a brief glimpse of someone rapidly closing one of the curtains in the bay window. It all happened far too quickly for me to see who had been looking at us, but it was enough to confirm that Justin was not alone in the house.

He must have noticed my momentary distraction. "What is it?" he asked.

"I'm sorry. Somebody was at the window there." I tilted my head in the direction of the bay. "That's all. Sorry."

"It was probably Mrs Greatorix – our cleaner. The job description I gave you may have implied that I keep the house single-handed, but I do get some help. I employ a gardener as well. Most of my time is taken up managing his financial affairs." Then he added with a mischievous grin, "Now, I feel sure you won't want me to go into his financial affairs."

I was not certain what he meant by this, but I took it as a warning not to pursue his involvement with the owner of the house. I said nothing, waiting to see if he was prepared to help me with Courtney's whereabouts.

"Mr Courtney is not a well man," Justin started to explain haltingly, searching for the right form of words. "Life has become ... difficult for him. He is being cared for in a home. I will give you the address."

"What sort of home – a psychiatric home?" I queried.

Justin hesitated briefly before agreeing. "Yes. I suppose it is."

"I'm so sorry," I said. "Is he ... very bad?" It was my turn to search for the right words. "Is he ... aware of things, what's going on around him?"

"Oh yes. Sometimes he is quite lucid. At others ..." he hesitated, "not so much. I see him regularly once a week – to get my instructions, for him to sign documents, and so on. I usually speak to one of the doctors to see how he's progressing."

"I'm confused," I said. "I've been told that he rented a house in Italy – just a few weeks ago."

"Yes," Justin said slowly, guarded. I knew I had touched a difficult subject for him. I had to proceed carefully.

"It wasn't for him then? He didn't go himself?" I queried.

"I'm sorry. I can't say any more. I value my position here, and I've already said too much. If you want to know any more, you'll have to get it from Mr Courtney direct. Wait here a moment please."

With that, he turned swiftly on his heels and went back into the house. He had not invited me in, so I waited in the porch, looking around at the extensive and well-tended gardens.

It was not long before he emerged and handed me a small sheet of paper. "Here's the address and telephone number for the home. It's about a quarter of an hour's drive. Their visiting hours don't start until two o'clock in the afternoon, so you've got time for a spot of lunch."

"OK," I said. "Look – many thanks, Justin. I do appreciate it." We shook hands, and I walked off to my car saying, "Great garden ... very nice."

I had not taken to the man. He had been very guarded in everything he said, but at least he had extended my lead. I took his parting advice and stopped off at a pub on the way to the nursing home. Over a beer and a sandwich, I considered how to approach the coming meeting. I suppose I have been fortunate, but I have had no experience in dealing with mental illness, and I felt curiously uneasy – unsure of what to expect. I may well have just one chance to get an answer from him, and I would need to treat Mr Courtney very carefully – respectfully, however the illness affected his behaviour.

At the stroke of two o'clock, I entered the home through a set of tall wrought iron gates. The short drive led to a rather bland modern red brick building, where a large sign ushered me into a sizeable visitor's car park. An elderly woman rose from her seat behind the reception desk and welcomed me with a disarming smile. Sporting a mound of blue-tinted hair and large pop eyes, she reminded me of Marge Simpson. A string of red beads clinging to her neck made me wonder whether the likeness was one that she was happy to cultivate.

"You're bang on time, young man," she said jauntily. "And who will you be visiting today?"

The formalities took rather longer than I had expected and, at one stage, it seemed that she might refuse my visit without some more formal introduction, but she accepted me as soon as I explained that Justin had directed me there. "Oh. Such a nice young man," she exclaimed. She went on to set out the routine for such visits. She would take me to the lounge, where tea would arrive for both of us. She would then fetch Mr Courtney and introduce him. He was a harmless old chap, she asserted, but was subject to quite wild mood swings. "And don't pay too much attention to what he says. He makes things up. You'll see."

I had a rather nervous wait in the lounge, which was furnished with a number of small tables surrounded by comfortable chairs, many of which were already occupied. I suddenly realised I had no idea how to refer to these people – patients, guests, inmates? I would have to avoid the subject in conversation. They were generally part of the older generation, of course, and many of them displayed odd movements and habits, some pulling funny faces at me. I tried to ignore them and kept a smile on my face. At one point, a younger woman got up from her chair and started towards me, muttering and smoothing down her clothing. I began to panic, but a member of staff in a crisp white tunic stepped forward and gently, but unobtrusively, steered her back to her table. So what should I call the staff – attendants, nurses ... guards?

Some men begin to die as soon as they retire. Others, in their eighties, remain much too interested in life and remain vigorous, always looking forward to the next decade. Mostly, this shows in their bodies and faces, but I have always had difficulties in assessing the age of older people. And so it was with Robertson Courtney as he approached with Marge. I guessed he was probably in his mid-sixties, but his most prominent feature was a shock of pure white hair. His face better evidenced his age, lined and craggy – but aristocratic, he would have been a handsome man in his youth. As he came close, he moved in front of Marge and offered me his hand saying, "Bill, how good of you to come."

This threw me for a moment. I had no idea how to respond and looked past him for help. Marge still had the same smile on her face, and the silence lingered until eventually, Courtney himself broke it with a giggle and, "Got you! I was just kidding." After a short pause, his face now serious, he challenged, "Do I know you?"

"No. We've never met," I confirmed. "My name is Martin Ramsay, and I'm very pleased to meet you. Let's sit and have some tea, Mr Courtney."

"Please. Call me Bob. Everybody does."

"Right! Mine is Martin. OK?" With introductions over, Marge began to move away slowly, and I began to wonder how to broach the only question I had for him.

"I've had quite a job finding you." I decided to slide in slowly.

"Oh yes?" He seemed surprised. "Well, you have done now. How may I help you?"

"It's about a property in Italy – on Lake Tousle" ..."

"The House in the Lake," Bob cut in triumphantly, as if it had won him a prize.

"Yes. That's the one. I was there a couple of weeks ago. It's a beautiful place."

"It surely is," he agreed. "Why the hell do you think I bought it?"

"You purchased it? It belongs to you?" I asked, incredulous.

"Sure! A long time ago now. My memory is not good these days but ... at least ten years ago."

"But I got your name from the Agency. You were listed as renting it four or five weeks ago."

"*Ouf*. I don't know anything about that," he said in a disinterested manner. "I have someone to deal with all that sort of thing for me."

"Justin. Yes. I've met him. He didn't say anything about you owning it."

"Ah well. It's not up to him to say. It's my business – not his. Come to think of it, why am I telling you all this? What's your interest in it? Are you going to make me an offer for the house?"

"No. I'd like to, but I could never afford it," I said with a short laugh. "No. I was out there a couple of weeks ago, and I met a girl there. Then something odd happened in the property – it's not quite clear what. But I'm trying to find out whether anything has happened to her."

"Aha. An affair of the heart, eh? I like that."

"Well," I started lamely. "I don't know about that. I only met Selene just once ..."

"*Who*?" Courtney cut in with a loud booming voice, and I could see heads around us turning. "Who did you say?"

The strength of his reaction shook me, and I briefly lost my voice. After a second or two, I managed, "She introduced herself as Selene."

"*Selene*," he broke in again, shouting. "What the fuck was she doing there?" With that, he sprang from his chair and flipped over the table, sending all the tea things flying. Staff appeared running from all directions and overpowered him impressively quickly.

Marge Simpson eventually arrived as they led him away. The smile had disappeared from her face as she turned to me. "What on earth did you say to him," she demanded.

I was shaken. How could I explain it? I didn't know what had set him off.

"I'm so sorry," was all I could offer. "I must have said something – I just mentioned a name. I have no idea what it was all about. I'm sorry."

"And this was the first time you'd met him?"

"Yes," I said.

"Well, I trust it'll be the last."

"It certainly looks like it," I agreed.

"Oh well," she said through pursed lips. "I'll see you out."

Chapter 9

I sat quietly in the car for some while, taking stock. I had learned several new things, but I could not immediately see how they would advance my cause. I decided that I needed to call again at the Courtenay house to speak some more with Justin, but it was now midway through the afternoon and I had a two-hour drive in front of me. I was accustomed to being home for Angie when she arrived from work but then reminded myself that I was now a free agent, and I could stay out as late as I wished.

Justin came to the door much quicker this second time. "I thought you'd be back," he said, and then rather wearily, "You had better come in."

He stood back against the door to shepherd me through. The hall was imposingly large, with a sweeping staircase leading up to a minstrel gallery. It was perhaps not as grandiose as one sees in Hollywood films, but impressive nonetheless, and he led me diagonally across it to another surprise. The building was undoubtedly old, and its character had largely been maintained, but as I entered the room that appeared to serve as the heart of the household, I could see that much of the rear had been opened up to form a vast, modern kitchen/diner. On the far side, a wide bay with french doors leading onto the garden was furnished with a coffee table and a couple of comfortable chairs.

"It's a bit early I suppose, but can I offer you a drink – or a cup of tea perhaps?" I thanked him and explained the circumstances under which I had already enjoyed less than half a cup, but declined any more.

"Not too successful a visit then?" he chanced.

"It certainly didn't end well, but I did learn a couple of useful pieces of information. For a start, I had no idea that he owns the house on the lake. You never told me that."

"Not my place to do so," he said lazily, to which I simply nodded my acceptance.

"But he's listed as renting the property in the agency's books. Why would that be?"

Justin shrugged. "I don't know if Sharon is even aware that he's the owner. She pays the rent straight into a nominee account – not to him directly. She may have guessed, of course, because of her instructions to waive the rent whenever it's booked in his name."

"Yes, he says that he has nothing to do with the bookings now. So presumably you make them all?"

"That's right. I do virtually all his paperwork. When Selene wants it, I have to reserve it in his name, of course. I can't book it in hers – you've seen for yourself his reaction to the idea of Selene being there."

"May I ask who Selene is then?"

The baldness of the question forced a moment of silence. "You may ask," he said eventually, "but I'm afraid that's more classified information. I'm sorry."

"She's some sort of relative, isn't she – his daughter perhaps." I did some lightening arithmetic in my head and added, "or even granddaughter … "

Justin's reaction provided me with a fresh view of the man. He had struck me as a rather dour individual, but this remark forced him to rock backwards with loud, uninhibited laughter. It died slowly and he was still chuckling as he explained, "Yes. They are indeed related, Mr Ramsay. But I assure you she's not his granddaughter, nor even his daughter. She is his wife!"

His words struck me dumb. The thought had never crossed my mind, and several seconds passed before I could summon up anything suitable to say.

"She told me she was unmarried," I said eventually, "although she did imply that she had been married at some time. Are they still married then?"

"Yes. I can confirm that. But I am saying no more."

"So her name is Selene Courtney?"

"Yes, I suppose it is. But I believe she also uses her maiden name – Grenville"

"Well, thank you for all that, Justin. I do appreciate it." I paused briefly. "I don't wish to push my luck, but I wonder if you would perhaps just give me your opinion. Why did he react so violently when I told him she was there on the island?"

"Oh, he has violent mood swings – all the time. It's a symptom of the illness." He thought for a while, and then added, "He's still very much in love with her, I guess. He gives her all the funds she needs – and they are considerable. And he gets virtually nothing in return. I assume, perhaps, he was upset at the thought of her at his house without him. They must have enjoyed many happy times there in the past. That may well have brought it on."

I simply nodded. I could not afford to push him further and might need to come back later for more information.

"I'll show you out," Justin said. I pushed back my chair. I was to be shown the door again – the second time in one afternoon.

We shook hands at the front door and, hoping to catch him off guard, I asked, "Do you know where she is now? Is she alive and well?"

He smiled but shook his head. "I have already said far too much. I will say nothing more, Martin. Goodbye, and good luck."

As I turned to go, he began to close the door. But then he reopened it a small way and said briefly, "If you're determined, Martin, my advice would be to ... Cherchez l'Italien. Goodbye."

As I drove home (for the moment, I felt I could still call it my home), I considered what I had learned from the day. Certainly, there were some useful fragments of information, but some were unexpected and others unwelcome. I felt vaguely dissatisfied –

disappointed. In part, this was no doubt due to the discovery that Selene was married. But why should this concern me? Her marriage was dead and buried – even deeper than my own.

The longer I thought about it, the more I realised that I was no nearer to finding Selene, nor even to discovering what fate had befallen her. And the longer I left it, the colder the trail would get. I would have to return to Italy – the place from where she had disappeared. Justin had reinforced this urge with his parting words, "Look to the Italian".

But which Italian, I wondered? Pino, or perhaps one of her fellow socialites.

Angie had already eaten by the time I got in, and I helped myself from the fridge. She made no mention of my late appearance, nor did she enquire where I had been. This may have been to avoid the possibility of a scene, but perhaps she had simply given up caring. Either way, I was grateful, and the evening passed without incident.

During the following day, I prepared the schedule of assets I had promised for Angie's solicitor. Once I had mailed it to her, I knew it would be several weeks before I was needed for the next stage of the divorce, so I set about planning a trip to Italy. There would be no arguments from Angie. She would assume I would be simply working on the house, and it would free us from the uneasy and somewhat surreal atmosphere with the two of us living together, but apart, in the same house.

I can easily lose myself in work. Indeed, it had already been one of the causes of the marriage breakup. And so it was in Italy, as I immediately threw myself into a variety of tasks. We had agreed to take down the ceiling in the living room, which would open it up into the roof, and I decided to tackle this next. I had already accepted that Angie should have the marital home, and it would make sense to make this property my home – at least for a while. If it was to be more than a simple summer holiday retreat, I felt it would be worthwhile increasing the quality of build, and quite possibly the amount of living space.

Except on the days I visited the town for supplies, this left me largely alone, and the solitude gave me ample time to indulge in my obsession with Selene. Those of you who have never been besotted in this manner will no doubt find it difficult to imagine the feeling of elation, but also the anguish, which is involved. The heady mixture of joy and disappointment plays havoc with the emotions, and it can become dispiriting unless some sign of possible fulfilment emerges. And any resolution for me seemed as far away as ever.

In the local bar, Angie and I had met and befriended another English couple who had moved permanently to Italy and had bought a lakeside house a few kilometres to the south. Mike and Barbara Robinson were a good twenty years older than us, but we got on well. Barbara in particular had made great efforts to master the language, but in the time they had lived in Italy, they had both gained a much better knowledge of the language, the people and their bureaucracy than we had. I decided to enlist their help and made a phone call arranging for them to come up for drinks at noon on the following day. No doubt, they would be sad at the news of our marriage breakup, and I was uncertain as to how they would react to my story of Selene. But if they were unable to assist me any other way, at least they could help me drink the afternoon away.

And that is pretty well all we did. I felt too uneasy to convey the extent of my obsession with Selene, and they felt that the local police should handle the matter. If they could not solve the mystery, what chance had I? Where should I even start? I had no answer to this, and all I achieved was a promise of help with translation when needed.

Several days passed and the new ceiling began to take shape nicely. As I worked, the usual fantasies involving Selene were interspersed with thoughts about my marriage problems, and some homespun philosophy. Nothing in life proceeds in a straight line, I mused. The replacement of our milk teeth, school and the turbulent teenage years, the choosing of a soulmate and the propagation of the species – the whole procession of life's events, they all progress in fits and starts, as had my current quest. And now it had stalled once again.

I could not possibly have foreseen the circumstances in which it would soon be revived.

Chapter 10

I have never been accused of appearing overdressed, favouring comfort over style. This frequently gives me a tumble-dried appearance, and it extends into my grooming. The current dishevelled style for hair comes naturally to me and suits me very well, but it does require that it is not too long. After a couple of weeks, without Angie to give it a trim, I realised that I would have to visit an Italian barber. I scoured the town and settled on one that did not appear too trendy, wondering how I was going to explain in sign language what I wanted.

As I entered, a couple of elderly men were waiting and gave me polite nods as I sat down to await my turn. It seems that waiting rooms are the same the world over. A collection of uncomfortable-looking chairs lined two of the walls. In front of them, a low table was strewn with untidy piles of magazines offering advice on buying houses and cars, dressing stylishly or decorating homes and gardens. Some of them were torn and many of them looked considerably out of date. Flipping idly through one that resembled an Italian version of Hello magazine, I must have spotted something subliminally, for I suddenly turned back a page and stared at it incredulously. It contained a series of photographs of society figures at a horse race meeting. But my eyes immediately focussed on one particular shot, and to a tall man elegantly dressed in formal clothes and a grey top hat. Something about him had struck me and I held the page closer to examine his face. I recognised the man. I was certain. It was Pino – or it was his identical twin brother.

"Cherchez l'Italien" – Justin's parting words. Was this "l'Italien" that he meant?

"Signore," I heard. The barber was calling to me. It was my turn. I threw the magazine back on the table and climbed into his chair. I made some elaborate hand signals until he got the message that all I needed was a trim. As he clipped away, I became increasingly worried that one of his waiting customers would pick up the magazine, and I kept peering at it in the mirror in front of me. I was determined to get hold of it somehow. New clients were arriving all the time and I realised I would never be able to conceal it without someone spotting me. It would be embarrassing, and I resolved to offer to pay for it.

It seemed an age before the barber brushed down the clippings and swished away the apron with the flourish of a bullfighter's cape. I picked up the magazine as he gently guided me over to the till. Once I had paid for the haircut, I made suitable gestures by holding the magazine in one hand and a one Euro piece in the other. He seemed to understand my offer but waved away the coin as he nodded acceptance and ushered me to the door, triumphantly holding my copy of Italian Hello.

My throat felt dry. I sat down in a pavement bar and ordered a beer, getting some odd looks as I spread out the magazine in the sun and carefully studied the page again. There was very little text, but I searched it for a mention of Pino's name. I could see nothing, and soon decided it was a job for Barbara Robinson.

I was just about to put it away, when I spotted something new, blinked and held it up even closer to my eyes. To the right of Pino, stretching up from the ground to well above his knee, I could make out a grey ribbed object, which I very quickly realised was part of a wheel's tyre. Above it, resting on a short platform, I could make out a hand along with an arm and shoulder, all unclothed. I guessed instantly that the object was a wheelchair, and I knew – I knew for certain – that Selene would have been sitting in it.

I cannot expect you to understand, nor even perhaps to believe, that my immediate reaction was just as I recall it today. This small cameo, this tiny portion of her naked flesh, made my heart leap. I had fantasized about Selene so often over the last few weeks, and here was a photo of her, albeit only a fragment.

Almost immediately, I wondered whether the magazine's editorial staff had cropped the picture from a larger original. But whether they had or not, it proved to me that she was alive. At least I had accomplished the first part of my mission.

But then, almost as quickly, I realised that this was a leap too far. Even if my presumptions were correct, and it was indeed a wheelchair holding Selene, I had no idea when the photograph was taken. I quickly turned to the front cover of the magazine, but there was no date – simply an issue number. I had more detective work to do.

I had another lead. A sense of excitement was rising in my stomach, which urged me to follow it up immediately, and I downed my beer quicker than I had intended. On the way home, I found the Robinsons out, so I settled down to a session with Google. The magazine itself was not online, but the publishers had a comprehensive website, which provided me with some contact numbers.

I dislike telephoning when I am abroad, particularly in Italy where the natives seem to speak less English than in the rest of Europe, and not for the first time I wondered how we had ended up in the country. The first number I called produced a flurry of "non capisco" mutterings until an operator was eventually found who could offer some hope of understanding me. I explained, slowly and deliberately, that I was trying to get a copy of a photograph published in Edition 132. I have no idea how much she understood, but it was sufficient for her to say charmingly, "Is possible maybe. I have to transfer telephone to new person. Maybe they help you."

The line seemed to go dead and I feared the worst. But after a while and the usual couple of clicks, a new voice cut in, "Hello. My name is Gizella. You are English. Yes?"

"Yes," I agreed, very relieved. "How much have you been told?"

"Nothing much," she said. "Simply that you wish for someone to speak in English. How can I help you?"

"I have just seen a copy of edition 132 and spotted a photograph of a friend. I am hoping that it could have been cropped from a larger picture, which might include some other friends. Is it possible to buy a copy please?"

"Oh, I'm sorry. That is most unlikely. We do not usually allow photographs out of the office. But it could depend on who was the photographer. What was the subject please?"

"It was at a horse race meeting. It's on page 23."

"I'll check it for you. Please hold the line for a little time."

"OK," I agreed. It was a blow. I would have to try to persuade her somehow. I could not let the opportunity slip.

She was gone for quite some time before she picked up the phone again. "Yes. It is what I thought," she started. "The series was taken by one of our in-house photographers. They cannot leave this office."

"Please. Is it possible in any way? It's very important to me."

"I'm sorry. It's not possible – policy of the Company."

I thought for a moment, and then asked, "Well, could you tell me about one of the photos, please? Do you have a copy of Edition 132 in front of you?"

"Yes. I do," she confirmed.

"On page 23, in the second photo from the left, third row, is there a girl in a wheelchair in the complete picture?"

There was a long pause before she replied, "Yes, there is. She is sitting beside Barone Guiseppi."

"*What*!" I exclaimed. "Who is she with?"

The girl at the other end of the line was silent, perhaps shaken by the strength of my reaction. Eventually, she sounded surprised, "Barone Guiseppi Morandi," she repeated.

"Who is he?" I asked. "Should I know him?"

"You said he was a friend of yours," she countered, regaining some of her composure. When I made no reply, she added, "He is very well known."

"OK." I paused for thought, and then continued, "If I can't have a copy, I guess that's all I can do. But thanks for your help. You speak excellent English, by the way."

"Thank you, sir."

I was just about to say goodbye and put down the phone when I had a sudden thought and asked, "By the way, edition number 132 – what date was it published?"

After another short pause, she announced, "It was the May edition, Sir – published towards the end of April."

My heart sank. With editorial and printing work, photographic material for this edition would have been taken in March at the very latest, so it was no proof that Selene was alive. I thanked her again and rang off.

Gizella was correct. Barone Guiseppi Morandi proved to be a very popular man indeed, and an internet search produced multiple pages of entries. I made notes as I read them from the top until a composite picture of him gradually emerged. He was the only son born to an old and revered Italian family that had for many generations been at the forefront of the country's racehorse breeding fraternity. When his father died, Guiseppi had inherited not only his title, the stud farm and considerable wealth but also his father's love of horses and his skills in rearing and preparing them for the racetrack.

Guiseppi had been married just once when he was still in his teens, but it had lasted only a few months. After that, whether by accident or design, he had steered well clear of lasting relationships and had become tagged as one of Italy's most eligible bachelors. His looks were hardly from the George Clooney mould, but he was a big muscular man with swarthy good looks, marred only by over-heavy jowls. He was always immaculately dressed and extremely rich, so that very few months went by without the paparazzi snapping him with some new beauty of screen, sport, music or simply notoriety itself. And there was almost no limit to the number of Italian publications willing to pay well for these pictures and stories.

My initial elation at discovering Pino, or Guiseppi as I now knew him, was wearing decidedly thin. He was no servant or medical supporter for Selene, but why was he willing to act the part? I found myself forced to accept that he was, in all probability, Selene's lover. And that, of course, set up a nagging sense of jealousy in me.

I had to find out more about the photograph. Gizella had confirmed that the photo included a girl in a wheelchair, and logic told me it must be Selene. But I had to be sure. And if it was she, how long had they been in a relationship? Indeed, if she was alive, were they still?

I had run into a brick wall at the Magazine's offices but wondered if the police might have more luck. If they were prepared to make a formal request, perhaps a claim for vital evidence, maybe they could obtain a copy for me. I dug out Inspector Grimaldi's card once more and telephoned him for an appointment. Within Italy, it turned out to be a direct line as he answered it himself, but as soon as I announced my name, I noticed a guarded tone enter his voice. Only when I insisted that I had uncovered new evidence did he reluctantly agree to see me.

I had not met him at his offices before and had always envisaged him seated in some small dingy office behind a large wooden desk covered with piles of dusty files. It was a surprise, therefore, when I found myself a couple of days later entering a smart new office block equipped with airport-style security. After a phone call from Reception, he came down and greeted me, "Good morning, Signor Ramsay."

He led me to his office, which was certainly not large, but was bright and cheerful. The modern impression was further enhanced by an array of computers and other electronic devices ranging around the room and on the desk behind which he seated himself.

"Well now, Signore. As I told you before, I have closed my file on this case. You will need some very good new evidence for me to open it again. What have you got for me?"

A stern uncompromising look accompanied this aggressive opening, but I was determined that I should not be fobbed off too easily. Before I took the seat opposite him, I slipped the magazine in front of Grimaldi and pointed to the photograph of Guiseppi. "That's the man I told you about on the island with Selene," I said.

Grimaldi leant forward to look and then picked it up to study it more closely. After a short while, he threw it back on the desk and leaned back in his chair. Placing the tips of his fingers together to form a tunnel of arches, he looked at me sourly, and with a slight shrug of his shoulders, he said simply, "So?"

I had expected him to show some surprise, and much of the wind had been taken from my sails, but I continued, "I'm guessing that you do recognize the man. Yes?"

"Of course. It is Barone Guiseppi Morandi. He is constantly pictured in this sort of rag."

"But look!" I shot up out of my seat. "Look here. This is part of a wheelchair. I am almost certain that Selene is sitting in it ..."

"But how does that help, Signore?" He cut in wearily. "Even if it is the lady who has stolen your heart, please do not let her steal your mind as well. The Barone is well renowned for his liaisons with beautiful women. If you're right about it being a wheelchair, and that it is your girl sitting in it, then all the picture proves is that the two of them were together at a race meeting at some time in the past." With that, he turned to the front of the magazine. "When was this published?" he wondered aloud.

"It isn't dated," I explained. "But I telephoned their office and it seems to have been published in April or May."

"Then the photo was taken well before the time you met them. It proves nothing." As he spoke, he was making some notes, as I suppose every police officer must. As he wrote, he flipped between pages of the magazine and then passed it back to me saying, "I can't help you, my friend. It changes nothing. I'm sorry."

"What I'm after is a copy of the original photograph. They wouldn't let me have one – claimed that it was company policy never to let in-house photos leave the building. I thought you might have more power – that you might be able to persuade them. I just want to make sure it was Selene that was with him."

Grimaldi shook his head. "No. No. I can't use any special police powers for that sort of thing. And besides, the case really is now closed. I'm sorry." He emphasised the point by physically closing his file with a thump, getting up and walking towards the door. The meeting was over, but before I left, I did manage a reluctant word of thanks to him for seeing me.

Disappointed, I returned home to a lonelier place than the one I had left. Once again, I threw myself into the work on the house, but the good progress I was making failed to satisfy me as it should. As I worked, I took stock of the situation. I now knew that Selene was a married woman and that she had taken a member of the Italian aristocracy as a lover. I was also aware that she was not averse to playing games with men such as me. If I had any sense at all, I should walk away and give up all thoughts of Selene.

And that is precisely what I decided to do.

Chapter 11

The postman had always been a stranger to us in Italy. Naturally, we had established a postal address, but nobody had written to us there, and we had arranged for all invoices for local taxes and utilities to be sent directly to England. It was a surprise, therefore, when he suddenly turned up three times in a single week.

He was a short stocky man with a ruddy round face that readily cracked open into a wide smile and a nervous tic that forced a blink every few seconds from one of his dark brown eyes. On his first visit, he seemed to be excited that he had managed to find our house, and talked at great speed in a high-pitched squeaky voice. Of course, I could not understand a word. With my limited Italian and him twitching away, I had no idea whether he was telling me a joke, asking me a question or merely passing the time of day. I smiled and nodded in a friendly effort to communicate, but with silence and a few gestures from me, he eventually got the message, closed down his mouth and handed me a large brown paper package.

I groaned inwardly as I opened it up to find a bundle of forms for me to complete, accompanied by a covering letter from Angie's solicitor. I put it to one side for my attention that evening, almost anything being preferable to the interminable game shows on Italian television.

The following day a letter arrived which I opened as soon as the postman had left. It was from Angie herself who started with a rather too-late warning that I would shortly receive some forms to be completed and signed. She then put into words her sadness at the failure of our marriage, and once again apologised for her infidelity. "You did not deserve it," she wrote. I was saddened and determined that I would tomorrow compose a reply in a similar vein.

Later that week, it seemed that yet more forms had arrived. I was in the process of damp-proofing the small cellar and my body was covered in the thick tar-like membrane when the postman arrived. I held up my black hands and pointed to a small table in the hall on which he placed down the parcel with exaggerated care, and gave me a weak smile as he left. I was in the middle of a job that I could not interrupt, taking only a very short lunch break, so I did not get around to opening the package until after I had finished supper. It was thin, but very firm. As I tore it open, it seemed to consist merely of a couple of pieces of stiff cardboard, but as I prised them apart, three large black and white photographs spilt out onto the dining room table.

I jumped out of my seat as I saw the first one – it was an un-cropped copy of the photograph in the magazine. And I had been right. Staring up at me was Selene, sitting in her wheelchair with her head turned, smiling up at her Barone. My sombre mood lifted immediately, and I swiftly glanced at the other photos. One was a full-face close-up of Guiseppi. The other was similar to the first but with a more serious Selene, looking to the front. I shook the pieces of cardboard for some sort of note, but there was none. I looked at the postmark and the back of the envelope. There was no indication of who had sent it. But I knew it could only have been Grimaldi. He had somehow arranged it anonymously. I would respect that, and silently offered up a private word of thanks.

Looking back now, I am not sure why these photographs immediately re-ignited my desires. It might simply have been the sight of her lovely face. Maybe it was the spectacle of her vulnerability, seated in her wheelchair. But perhaps it was concern over how her Italian lover had treated her. Had he attacked her? Had he killed her? Not for the first time, I steeled my resolve to discover the truth.

Several entries from my Google search had revealed the location of the Morandi estate, but I could hardly march in and accuse the Barone of murder. I needed to devise a careful plan. Over the next few days, I formed and discarded some rather contrived scenarios, but finally settled on a simpler, more direct approach.

A couple of days later, I found myself driving along a sun-bleached stony track, lined by Cypress trees, that made its way over undulating hills into the heart of the Morandi estate. It was nearly five minutes before I came across the family's house, in front of which were parked a number of expensive-looking cars.

It was a large house, but plain – lacking the porticos, pillars and other decorative features of some of the more elaborate buildings I had seen in the country. Under the vernacular shallow pantile roof, there were just two stories built of a light golden stone, peppered with windows framed by pale blue shutters. It was a wide building and, at either end, sported a small wing that reached forward a few metres from the middle section. In the centre, a wide stone staircase led up to a large open doorway on the upper floor, and it was from here that an elderly lady appeared as I got out of the car. Her white hair contrasted sharply with the severe black dress she was wearing, but she descended the stairs sprightly enough and walked to greet me.

"Buon giorno, Signore."

"Buon giorno," I managed. "Parla Inglese?"

"No. Mi dispiace."

This was not going to be easy, I decided. "Guiseppi Morandi?" I tried.

She shrugged, lifted her arms with her hands spread wide, and then beckoned to me to follow her. She led me around to a terrace at the side of the house and pointed to a cushioned rattan chair beside a matching table, I presumed to await Morandi. After about five minutes, she returned from the back of the building with a welcome cup of coffee. "Grazie", was one of the few other words in my Italian dictionary.

It was very pleasant, sitting in the morning sunshine, as I slowly enjoyed my coffee and rehearsed the conversation I hoped to have shortly with Guiseppi. It was some twenty minutes before a group of horses and riders breasted a grassy ridge and trotted towards the terrace. Most of the horses were breathing heavily and glistening with sweat from the morning gallop, but my eyes became fixed on the large leading horse, and on its rider who dwarfed all the other jockeys.

Guiseppi, wearing jodhpurs and a loose white shirt, appeared totally at ease in the saddle as he approached. I saw him frown as he caught sight of me, but he continued with the others towards the stable block that lay some hundred metres or so behind the house. Suddenly, however, he pulled up sharply, eased his feet out of the stirrups, lifted his right leg over the saddle and slipped to the ground – all in one smooth and well-practised movement. He looked puzzled, perhaps a trifle worried, as he came up to me.

"Dove ci siamo conosciuti?" he asked, unsure.

"I'm sorry," I reacted. "I don't speak much Italian. But I know you speak English."

As I spoke, a look of comprehension spread over his face as he remembered where he had seen me. "Ah. I remember you now. Up north – the house in the lake."

"That's right," I said, and offered my hand, "Martin Ramsay."

He was still looking concerned, clearly working through the implications of my visit. He said nothing but almost grudgingly took my hand with a slight nod. We stood facing each other for a few seconds, like a couple of gunfighters sizing up each other's speed on the draw.

Eventually, Guiseppi broke the silence. "You've chosen a bad day, my friend. I have a meeting right now. In fact, I see from the cars that people have already arrived, and I'm late. I cannot see you today. I'm sorry."

He then looked up to the sky, pensive, presumably seeking a mental picture of his diary. Suddenly, he met my eyes again and said, "Can you make it tomorrow morning at ten o'clock? I can give you half an hour."

"Yes," I agreed. "Thank you. I'll be here."

We briefly shook hands again and Guiseppi strode off hurriedly to his meeting. I stood rooted to the spot for a few moments, looking after him as he disappeared around the corner of the house. Was this Selene's man – the one I had met on the island? There was nothing servile about this version, and his command of English was impressive.

The estate lies less than twenty kilometres from the ancient Tuscan city of Lucca. When searching for a suitable place to stay, I had come across the Barone Hotel – a coincidence that I was unable to resist, and I had checked in the previous evening. It turned out to be a charming old family-run hotel deep in the heart of the old city, and I spent the day getting my bearings, wandering around the age-old streets, and enjoying an al fresco dinner in the Piazza dell'Anfiteatro.

The only problem with older city centre hotels can be the street noise, particularly at night. This hotel was not the worst in the world, but the racket was enough to delay my sleep, and the day's events churned over in my mind. One thing I was pleased about was Guiseppi's English. It appeared to be fluent – as one might expect of an international figure. Certainly, it was very different from the halting, heavily accented English I experienced when I last saw him. But I did wonder whether Guiseppi genuinely had a meeting, or whether he had merely invented it to postpone ours. Was he playing for time?

Another bright day and the sun streaking through the flimsy curtains woke me early. The morning traffic was heavier than I had expected and I found myself speeding to make our ten o'clock meeting. I was only around five minutes late, but the Barone was already waiting for me on the same terrace, looking rather stern. But he brightened up and smiled as I approached, and we exchanged "buon journos" and shook hands.

He was dressed, as on the previous day, in a loose shirt and jodhpurs. "I thought you might like a tour of the estate," he suggested. "Can you ride a horse?"

"No. I'm afraid not. I did once, in Ireland, but it wasn't a great success."

"I guessed not. We'll take the mule."

I immediately envisioned myself spending the morning following this tall man around the countryside on a donkey, like Sancho Panza. Guiseppi must have read my thoughts because he grinned and added, "A Kawasaki Mule. It's in the car park over there. Come on ..."

The all-terrain vehicle looked immaculate, brand new. There were no doors and, no sooner had we clambered into the single bench seat, than I felt my head rock backwards and my body sink into the seat's backrest as Guiseppi floored the accelerator. I started to laugh nervously as the Mule left the gravel car park and leapt onto a steep grassy slope. It was in its element now, running free and exhilarating.

Guiseppi must have given the same tour a thousand times, but he enjoyed showing off his domain. Every so often, he would pull up to show a particular feature. There were cottages for his workers, fields of hay almost ready for an early harvest, and any number of enclosures holding strings of the most elegant racehorses. After about ten minutes, he pulled into a copse where he explained his staff managed to provide all the wood that the estate needed – everything from fencing to firewood. A track led through to a small clearing where the trees had been felled and piled into giant stacks.

Guiseppi slammed on the brakes and the Mule slithered to a halt on the loose surface of pine needles. He sat back and stared ahead, silent.

"Let's talk about the house in the lake," he said eventually. "What can I tell you?"

"I'd like to know what happened there, Barone. I left you alone with Selene on that island, and when I returned a couple of days later, there was nobody there – nobody. The house was a mess – someone had trashed it. And there was blood all over the patio, and down the path – even in the boat." I paused briefly. "I want to know what happened."

Guiseppi did not answer immediately. He seemed unsure what to say but eventually gained some time with, "You went to the police. I heard." Then after a short pause, "They talked to me about it quite recently. I cannot afford to get involved, Signore."

"But you are involved. I saw you there with her. What the hell did you do to her?" It came out rather quickly – too much like an accusation. But I let it run.

Again, he took his time before answering. Eventually, he seemed to come to a decision. "OK. You will not like it, but I will tell you what happened." He paused before continuing. "What do you think happened? After all, you are involved too. You arrived and started flirting with Selene, and she responded – flirting back. I told her how pissed off I was with her behaviour, and we had a furious row about it that night.

After you'd left in the morning, she revived it and we never got to our meeting." He paused again.

"You don't know Selene. You probably see her as some sweet little wounded bird that can't look after itself. You'd be so wrong. She has a quick temper too, which she took out on me that day. She went mad – throwing things at me, charging at me with the wheelchair. And she's strong. Believe me!"

After a moment's thought, he continued. "I am stronger, of course, and I should have been able to contain her, but she came at me with a large kitchen knife. I tried to fend her off and escaped onto the patio, but she kept coming on – like a mad thing. By now, I was losing my cool. I managed to get the knife from her, and then ... used it to stop her." He went silent.

"What do you mean," I demanded fearfully, *"used it to stop her?"*

He shrugged. "I stopped her. She was out of control, and I had to stop her. Believe me, I've played it over and over in my mind ever since. There was no other way."

"You're saying you stabbed her?" I demanded, incredulous.

Guiseppi simply nodded.

"How many times? Did you keep on stabbing her?"

"I don't remember. Everything's a haze. You don't need to know any more, Signore."

"I do need to know." I was beside myself now. "And the police will want every little detail."

He didn't seem to hear me. He certainly didn't answer me but continued, "She slid out of her chair. She just lay there, in pools of blood. Lots of blood."

He spoke with his hand over his face, unable to look at me. After a while, he continued, "I tried, but I couldn't stop the bleeding. I didn't have to feel her pulse. She was dead. I knew she was dead."

"I've been having nightmares about this," I said, breathless now. "It's just as I imagined. You took her body out in the boat and ditched it somewhere in the lake. Didn't you?"

"Something like that," he said softly.

Both of us fell silent then. What more was there to say?

"Where do we go from here?" I asked eventually. Guiseppi said nothing.

"We have to go to the police." I answered my own question. Again, there was no response, and I waited for a reaction. He was staring now, not at me, but far into the distance.

"Guiseppi," I shouted. "We have to go to the police ..."

This broke his trance and he cut in angrily, "I've told you, I cannot get involved." There was a short pause before he continued. "We get only one life, and mine is good. I will not have it cut short now." As he said this, he reached under the front dashboard and came out holding an evil-looking snub-nosed revolver.

"You should not have gone to the police, Signore," Guiseppi said quietly. "And now ... I'm sorry. Wrong time, wrong place."

He turned towards me. "Get out," he ordered brusquely.

It had all happened so quickly and so unexpectedly. A gun pointing at me was a new experience and at first, I was more surprised than frightened. But after a few seconds, the full extent of my grim situation hit me and I began to shake. My mind was racing. Why did he want me out of the vehicle? Because it was new and might be damaged? Unlikely. Guiseppi was much too wealthy to worry about such things. No, I suspected it was the risk of creating too much physical evidence. I decided I would be safer if I stayed in the Mule.

But Guiseppi repeated, "Get out of the car." He was shouting now. "*Out . . . now.*"

I stayed where I was. He transferred the gun to his left hand and started pushing me out with his other. My mind was running at top speed now. He had taken the gun out with his right hand – so was probably right-handed, I thought. With the gun in his wrong hand, I made a sudden decision and threw myself out of the Mule, scrambling up and starting to run past the back of the vehicle. A couple of shots rang out, more noisy than accurate.

Guiseppi could have leapt out his side, and I would have been an easy target. But I heard him starting up the Mule again. I headed for the nearest tree line. He would find it more difficult driving in the woods and the trees would offer me some degree of cover. As I ran into the copse, I heard another shot thud into a tree close to my head. I ducked involuntarily and started dodging in and out between the trees. I was breathing heavily already and wondered how long I would be able to last.

The Barone had abandoned the Mule now and was chasing on foot. I knew the odds were stacked against me. He was gym fit, whilst I was completely out of shape. It would not be long before he chased me down. I could see I was getting closer to the edge of the wood, and my cover would be gone. I changed direction to prolong protection from the trees, but the Barone saw me and cut off the angle, which further reduced the distance between us.

I was in a bad way now, and reaching the end. I knew I couldn't run much further. I was straining to force air into my lungs, my whole body swathed in sweat. I half turned to see how close Guiseppi was, but lost my footing and started to fall. As if in slow motion, I fell backwards landing on a soft bed of pine needles. I lay there, my chest heaving and my eyes closed, waiting for the sound that would mark my final despatch into oblivion. But the shot never came and after a while, I ventured ever so slowly to open my eyes.

I found myself staring at the hotel ceiling. As I lay there motionless, my chest gradually subsided into a slow pattern of panting. After around five minutes, my breathing was steady and the sweat had largely dried, now forming an extra layer of dry skin.

Very slowly, my mind returned to the real world and I tried to make sense of my dream. Was it a warning? Was I being stupid to confront the Barone? Would I be in danger in the morning? With no answers to these questions, I fell once more into a deep sleep.

Chapter 12

The sunshine glowing through the curtains contrasted sharply with the deep sense of foreboding that enveloped me. I still had no answers to the questions of the night, but no evidence sufficient to back away from my planned meeting. I took some note of the dream, however, and determined not to be late.

Sharp at five minutes to ten I rolled up in front of the Morandi house and could see that the Barone was already waiting for me, drinking coffee on the same terrace. As I approached, he poured me a cup from an insulated jug and then rose to greet me. Designer jeans had replaced the jodhpurs of the previous day, so I guessed he probably hadn't been out riding that morning. I recognised the dog that lay on the ground beside him, and who once again showed very little interest in my arrival.

After handshakes, Guiseppi waited for me to start the conversation, "That's the dog I saw at the lake, isn't it?"

"Yes, he is – Lucio. He goes everywhere with me." As he said this, he reached down and ruffled the top of the dog's head.

"Lucio. Yes, I remember," I said. "Speaking of names, what would you like me to call you? Apart from your title, I've heard you called Pino and Guiseppi, but perhaps you have another name you would like me to use?"

"I have a whole string of forenames, but I won't trouble you with them. Guiseppi will do fine," he smiled.

"Where does Pino come from?" I asked.

"It's a nickname – a friendly sort of thing. My name is sometimes elongated to Guiseppino, and it can then be chopped short again. My mother always called me Pino – still does, and my close friends." He paused briefly and then, getting down to business, "Guiseppi will do, Martin. How can I help you?"

Ominously, the conversation now began to resemble that of my dream. "I want to know what happened at the house in the lake. I left you with Selene and, when I went back a couple of days later, someone had trashed the place, and there was blood on the terrace, paths and boat. What happened to Selene?"

"Nothing happened to Selene," Guiseppi insisted.

The flat denial flummoxed me for a second or two. "What do you mean, *'Nothing happened to her'*? You mean she's alive and well. She's around somewhere?"

Guiseppi had been smiling throughout, and now said, "Yes, of course. She's around somewhere – JC will have seen to that."

I have heard other people use these initials, as shorthand to prevent blaspheming with "Jesus Christ" or "My God". It seemed slightly odd in this context, but I thought I understood what he meant. She enjoyed divine protection. She was fireproof.

"Well, I'm so pleased to hear you say that, Guiseppi." I was elated. He had lifted a huge weight from my mind. "But what was all the blood? She must have been injured in some way."

Guiseppi said nothing. He sat and stared at me for several seconds, but the smile was gone. Suddenly, he pushed back his chair, stood up and took a couple of steps backwards. My astonishment grew as he unbuckled his belt, unzipped his flies, and stood still as his jeans floated down around his ankles. A pair of powerful legs were exposed, each covered in a thick mat of black fur. I stared in amazement but then spotted a wide parting in the hair. A long swathe stretched from just above his right knee and disappeared up behind his shirttail. Guiseppi must have noticed the course of my eye movements for he lifted his shirt to reveal that it continued right up close to his crutch. And running down the middle of it was a livid scar, crossed every few millimetres by imprints left by a considerable number of stitches.

"Shit," was the only word that came to my mind, and from thence to my mouth.

Guiseppi dropped his shirttail and bent down to pull up his jeans. I waited until he had buckled his belt before I asked, "What happened then? Are you telling me that Selene did that?"

He sat down and took another slurp of coffee before he began, "She did ... but I don't believe it was intended. I have put it down to an accident – brought on by the furious row we were having." And after a short pause, "Actually, the row was about you."

"*About me?*" I queried immediately. What about me? You can't have been jealous – surely?"

This brought a smile back to his face. "No. No. It wasn't jealousy. You can't be jealous of a girl like Selene. She is a girl for the world – at least, the world of men. Anyway, I'm not a jealous sort of person." He took another slug of caffeine before continuing, "No, it was the game she played with you. I didn't like it. It wasn't fair. And I was annoyed with myself that I went along with it – and indeed, took part in it. It wasn't good, and I said so to her. She went wild."

He fell silent for a moment and then looked at me intently before he continued earnestly, "You don't know Selene, Martin. She's a lovely thing for sure, but she has such a temper on her."

Once again, his words were beginning to echo those of my dream, as Guiseppi continued, "And she likes to have her own way. You don't cross her – and never criticise her. I did that day, and it caused a mighty quarrel. All of a sudden, she started to throw things at me, and all around the place. I got angry myself and started smashing up some of the chairs. It just got totally out of hand."

"Eventually, she completely lost it and came at me with a knife. She chased me out onto the patio and started bashing into me with her wheelchair. I tried to wrestle the knife from her, but she has extremely strong arms and ... well, I don't know exactly what happened, but I hope it was an accident. I cried out as she cut me. She knew immediately what she had done and stopped instantly, beginning to cry. Through her tears, she started examining my leg to see the damage."

"She was sobbing uncontrollably as she left me lying on the ground and wheeled herself rapidly into the house. Moments later, she reappeared with an armful of towels and bandages, and together we managed to close the wound and bind it up tightly. The blood was still seeping through, but not pumping out as it had been."

"She'd called for an ambulance, but somehow we had to get to the mainland. Selene locked up the house and, by leaning on her chair, I managed to hobble down to the landing stage. Then we had to get her into the boat. That wheelchair folds, so that was easy enough, but Selene had to sit on the side of the stage for me to lift her in – she's very light. In the ten days we'd been there, we'd pretty well mastered the manoeuvre, but it was much more difficult with my leg, which had started bleeding badly again."

"It was all very painful, but we managed it somehow, then had to wait about ten minutes for the ambulance. In our panic, we'd forgotten Lucio who started howling pathetically, thinking we'd abandoned him. We called to him and he eventually took the plunge and swam to us, reaching shore just as the ambulance arrived." He leant over again and patted the dog with, "Brave boy."

"The paramedics examined me, bound my leg with a compression bandage and got me to the hospital. I had lost a lot of blood, but it could easily have been much more serious. They gave me a transfusion, patched me up and I was able to leave on crutches in a couple of days. And here I am, as you see, alive and well."

I had listened to the tale in silence, but still had a few questions. "Did you see her again after that?"

"No. I don't know whether she was afraid that I might start some criminal action, but as soon as I was safely in the hospital, she disappeared. No, I have not seen her since. A big bunch of flowers was delivered here with a brief apology on a card. But that's all."

"Do you know where she is?"

"No. I've no idea – and I don't care. Even before you arrived on the scene, our relationship was in its death throes. We both knew it, and that may explain all the attention she paid to you."

"So ... I take it you won't be taking any action against her?"

"No." Guiseppi shook his head. "I do believe it was an accident, and she's probably out of the country by now. Anyway, what good would it do?"

"Guiseppi, I can't tell you how relieved I am to hear all this," I told him. "I've had visions of her somewhere at the bottom of the lake."

"The mind can play funny tricks," he said. After a moment's thought, he continued, "You were very attracted to her, weren't you? She certainly is a fascinating woman – but beware, Martin. Beware."

Probably looking a bit sheepish, I said nothing.

Five minutes later, after thanks and goodbyes, I was on my way back to the hotel. I settled the bill and headed for home, a journey of some three hours or more. This gave me ample thinking time, and I found myself thankfully accepting the Italian's assurance that Selene was safe and unharmed. I was elated, with the first part of my mission ending happily. At the time, I don't believe I ever doubted his story. Certainly, she had injured him – quite seriously. But they were lovers presumably, and the row had been furious. Had it ended there?

Chapter 13

I was needed back in England. A letter from Angie's solicitor awaited me, telling me that additional details about our investments would be required before she could prepare the final divorce papers. I had none of this information in Italy and decided to travel back the following day.

But travel back to where? My mind had settled on this house in Italy as being my home, at least for the time being. I no longer had a home in England. Although I would undoubtedly have to call in at the family house, which was where I still held all my files, it was equally certain that I could not stay there anymore. This thought reminded me of something else I must soon organise – to move all my stuff out, possibly into temporary storage.

My mother died of cancer when I was only five years old. I have only the vaguest memories of her – all warm and cuddly. I may be biased, but I consider my father to be a remarkably handsome man. He has now lost the vast majority of his hair, but he has retained most of the finely chiselled features of his younger self and has managed to avoid adding too much spread to his tall frame.

He remarried only a few days after the first anniversary of my mother's death. I liked his new wife. We got on famously and she was glad for me to call her mummy. This continued happily until my early teens, but by this time she had fallen out with my father and I became witness to a daily round of alternate ferocious rows and suffocating silences. Inevitably, it ended in divorce – and I lost my second mother.

My father did not marry again – at least, not then. But he installed a new woman in the house almost as soon as the divorce was complete. I disliked her from the start and I am sure it was mutual, for we hardly ever spoke to one another. Oddly enough, I didn't blame my father, and in fact, became much closer to him. This developed still further when Janet left very suddenly and it was just the two of us again until I went to university. It was then several years before he met Stephanie, a very pleasant divorcee of about his age. They married after a while, and now live together on the Norfolk coast. Like all his previous women, she is attractive – small, with a crop of tightly curling grey hair, rosy cheeks and an infectious laugh.

I had kept well in touch with my Dad over the years, telephoning him every couple of weeks or so and visiting three or four times a year – sometimes with Angie and others alone. I had called him almost immediately to tell of my split with Angie. It had naturally upset him, but he was both understanding and sympathetic. All this set me to wondering if I should use him as my base in England – just until I could make other, more permanent arrangements. A telephone call gained an enthusiastic offer, "Of course, my boy. Stay as long as you like."

A couple of days later saw me enjoying dinner with both of them in the kitchen of their neat little cottage on the outskirts of Wells-next-the-Sea. My father had always been fond of Norfolk, frequently holidaying there with his various women. He was newly retired, and I was so pleased that he had finally found love and happiness in his declining years.

After my exploits in Italy, I was determined to spend two or three days relaxing and reconnecting with the family. My father had acquired a small boat, powered by either oars or a small outboard motor, which we took out each day pottering around the muddy lanes of the estuary or exploring the beaches along the coastline. Long walks with my father and his Labrador tired me out and I was happy to retreat to bed each evening immediately after the Ten o'clock News. Only then did I get the opportunity to work up mental lists of the tasks in front of me. At other times, I was surprised by the occasional snatched vision of Selene, rather like commercial breaks interrupting a domestic soap opera. I soon realised, almost reluctantly, that she retained firm possession of my heart – still the object of all my desires, despite Guiseppi's dire warnings. His cautions echoed around my brain, and I tried to banish her from my thoughts. But the visions kept recurring. Where was she now I wondered?

But for the moment, there was much else to occupy my mind, and I had to head south again.

I arranged to meet Angie at the house to sort out the information that her solicitor needed. But first, I would need somewhere to stay. I could think of no one suitable to land myself on. My soulmate had died several years earlier, and all my other local friends were jointly friends with Angie. Approaching any one of them could be construed as asking them to take sides, and I was not prepared to embarrass any of them in this way.

Then I remembered a hotel Angie and I had used for several weeks whilst I carried out work to the house before it was fit to occupy. I remembered it as usefully located, well-run and reasonably inexpensive. I telephoned and was able to reserve a room for a couple of weeks.

It was a weird feeling, ringing the bell of the home I had made – and for the moment still owned. I stood there, waiting for Angie to answer the door, all the time feeling unexpectedly nervous about meeting up with her. Perversely, it felt almost like a first date rather than one of the last. And when she opened the door with a smile, neither of us seemed to know what to do – shake hands, a small kiss perhaps. In the end, we did neither and I broke the ice with, "Hi Angie. How've you been?"

"OK, Martin. Come on in."

She made coffee and we sat round the kitchen table, as we had done so many times over the years. We talked of her work, my progress with the house in Italy and news of friends. It was more than half an hour before the conversation steered itself naturally to the subject of our divorce.

"Right," I started. "I got a letter from Miss Fairchild. She wants some more information about our investments. I thought we'd agreed on all the financial arrangements. You're not having second thoughts, Angie?"

"No. As far as I'm concerned, it's all agreed." She seemed genuinely surprised by my question.

"Fine," I said with a smile. "I expect it's just some technicalities. I'll go and get the information she wants."

As I set off towards my small study area, she called after me, "We'll take it along to her. She wants to see us both next week."

Half an hour later, I was still going through the files when Angie put her head round the door. "Fancy a spot of lunch?" she asked.

"Love some," I said. "That would be great. I've nearly finished – about a quarter of an hour?"

She scuttled off and I turned back to the small pile of documents. The figures were turning out pretty well along the lines of those I had already provided. But I was desperate to avoid any disputes or other problems, double-checking them all and making sure that I had included everything.

Lunch was not quite as relaxed as our earlier conversation. We talked easily enough but, after a while, some awkward pauses developed. After one such break, Angie reopened our previous discussion, "Miss Fairchild wants to bring us right up to date. Once she's incorporated your figures, she'll be ready to send you the final papers setting out the reasons for the divorce, the settlement of property, etc. After you agree to them, it'll be around a month before the Court hearing."

"OK. Have you made an appointment?" I asked.

"No," she said, getting up and heading for the telephone. "Let's do it now, while you're here."

We fixed a date for early the following week and then turned to other matters on my 'to-do' list.

"I'll have to find a flat or a house – somewhere to live. The Italian house is fine for now, but I can't believe I'll want to live there permanently."

"No. I don't suppose you will. You'll keep it though?" She looked up anxiously.

"Sure. It's the only home I have now, and I've decided to make it a bit bigger."

She nodded. "That's a good idea."

"But until I find somewhere permanent, I've got nowhere to store all my stuff. I'll take all the investment files with me today. I'll need to work on them over the next few days, and I'll have to cash in some of the investments to raise your money. But I looked around the study, and there's a whole lot of other stuff to be moved

– computers, CDs, DVDs, some of our photos," I shook my head, "And then upstairs, I've got loads of clothes I'll need. Where the hell am I going to store everything?"

"You don't have to move everything immediately," Angie, answered, almost in a whisper. "I won't throw anything away. Just get yourself sorted, eh."

"Thanks, Angie," a brief pause and then, "will you be going to the Court hearing?"

"Yes. I've thought about it, and I will."

"I agree. We'll go together," I said. It seemed right somehow. We were in church together for the marriage. We should surely be together to witness its end – a form of closure.

"Right!" I smiled at her, "I'll be off then. I've got a lot to do."

I did well that day. I managed to identify five investments that would yield sufficient to pay off Angie's lump sum and sent off the necessary applications to encash. I telephoned my father and got his permission to store some of my things in the spare bedroom. I also telephoned local agents for details of properties I might find suitable to rent. Selene hardly got a look-in that weekend. Indeed, several busy days would pass before she once again crept into my consciousness – and then only by chance.

I had been looking at properties all day and, after drinks and dinner in a restaurant, I returned late to my hotel. I was tired. I sat down in the only chair in my room and turned on the TV. At home, Angie and I had developed the habit of watching only recorded programmes, as there never seemed to be anything worth watching when we turned on the TV. But that night, my luck was in, and I caught the start of a film. Called *Shadow of a Doubt,* it was old, shot in black and white, but as the credits rolled, I was encouraged to see that it was directed by Alfred Hitchcock. Joseph Cotton plays Uncle Charlie, who arrives to stay for a while with his elder sister. His well-travelled sophistication is a great hit in the small American town, particularly with his sister's teenage daughter who quickly forms a crush on him. But two men are tracking him and one of them talks to the young girl, explaining that they are detectives. He warns her of their suspicion that her uncle is the dangerous killer that the press has dubbed the "Merry Widow Murderer." She refuses to believe him at first, but later observes Uncle Charlie acting strangely. Then she notes that the initials engraved inside a ring he gave her match those of one of the murdered widows. When he realises that she has become suspicious, her life is suddenly thrown into mortal danger.

It was whilst I was watching the movie that I experienced some niggling doubts. I managed to put them aside to enjoy the film, but they returned when I was in bed. Was Guiseppi living the same lie as Uncle Charlie? He had been convincing enough, but I had no actual proof that Selene was alive – only the Italian's word.

I must have tossed my suspicions around during the night, but only the clarity of a new dawn led me to thoughts of decisive action. Quite simply, I could only be certain that she was alive if I were able to see her with my own two eyes. I wondered if I might be kidding myself – that I was using it as an excuse to meet up with her again. But I decided to telephone Guiseppi, who must have known Selene for some time. If he were as innocent as he claimed, he would surely be able to give me some clues as to her possible whereabouts.

I knew Guiseppi's morning routine quite well and left my call until 9.30 our time when he would hopefully be back from exercising the horses. The Barone answered almost immediately.

"Ciao Guiseppi," I greeted him. "It's Martin here – Martin Ramsay. We met recently on your estate."

"I remember you, Martin. I thought I had answered all your questions," he said guardedly. "What more can I tell you?"

"I know, Guiseppi. You were very kind. But you know Selene well, and you know the places she likes to hang out. Can you think of anywhere she might be? I really would like to meet up with her again."

There was silence from the other end of the line. Eventually, Guiseppi said rather curtly, "You don't believe me, do you? You still want proof."

"No. No, Guiseppi," I insisted, embarrassed that I had been caught out. "Your leg ... I do believe you. I just want to see her again."

"You don't want to see her, Martin. I told you. She's bad news."

"Yes – I do remember what you said, and I'll bear it all in mind, I promise. But it's my life, and I have to go where my heart takes me."

I could imagine Guiseppi shrugging as he sat on the terrace with his morning coffee. "Ah well," he said finally. "As you say – it's your life. But I can't help you anyway. I have no idea where she is."

He paused for a moment or two, perhaps considering her favourite places, then added, "JC may know where she is – I certainly don't and, as I've already told you, I don't fucking care." Then, after a moment, he had listened to me long enough. "Arrivederci, Signor Ramsay," he said, and the line went dead.

Almost as soon as I had put the receiver down, it rang again. I jumped back to it, thinking that Guiseppi might have had a second thought, but it was Angie. She had heard from her solicitor that she was ready to serve the divorce papers, which she would send to me that day by courier. She had also agreed to a provisional date for the Court hearing in five weeks, provided I could agree on things quickly. I assured her there would be no delay on my part, and she was still on the line when there was a loud knock on my door. Cupping the phone under my chin, I opened it, and the hall porter thrust a large package into my hands.

"The papers have arrived," I told Angie, and then spent the rest of the afternoon studying their contents. I had to call Miss Fairchild to explain one or two legal points, but it was all reasonably straightforward, and I sent off my agreement before the end of the day.

Throughout my life, I have noticed that my best ideas seem to come to me in the bath. It may be the solitude, as it is frequently the first time that day when I am truly alone. Or it may be the womb-like comfort of the enveloping hot water. And so it was that evening, as I lay reviewing the day's events. For several hours, something had been niggling away at the back of my mind, and I eventually narrowed it down to my conversation with Guiseppi – something he'd said. All at once, it came to me. It was the second time he'd used the initials JC in place of Jesus Christ. Both times, it had somehow seemed slightly odd in the context.

Then the lightning struck. Was it possible? I'd have to check online. Unlike the ancient Greek, I did not immediately rush out of the bath shouting "eureka", but I did certainly curtail my normal lengthy soak. I fired up the computer again and excitedly googled "Jesus Christ in Italian". The answer came up almost immediately "Gesù Cristo". As I suspected – to an Italian, his initials would not be JC at all. For a moment, I wondered whether he might have anglicised it for my benefit – but I doubted it. So was he then offering me some sort of clue?

I went to bed with the letters J and C hovering around my lips. Were they perhaps the initials of somebody I knew? I had been pondering this for only a few minutes when the penny started to descend ever so slowly. The only person I could think of in the whole saga whose surname began with "C" was Selene's second husband, Robertson Courtney. He was surely unlikely to know Selene's whereabouts – half out of his mind in a psychiatric home. The man I had met in his house handled all his wife's reservations and other affairs. But this thought suddenly accelerated the penny's fall. Of course – Justin. Justin with a "J". Perhaps he was no mere employee. Could he be Robertson's son? If so, had Guiseppi known it and given me the clue? I gave him a mental nod of thanks.

The whole mystery was beginning to unravel in front of me. Justin had control of his father's affairs, possibly made through an Enduring Power of Attorney. It would certainly finance his lifestyle, and give him possession of the magnificent family home. Had he also taken possession of his wife? It would certainly make a very attractive base for her in England. This in turn led to another thought – the person I had briefly spotted twitching at the curtains on my first visit. It could have been the cleaner, but it might also have been Selene. Had she been living with Justin, their life together financed by his father?

I had visions of poor old Roberson, as I had last seen him in the nursing home, being dragged to his room by a pack of tough-looking male nurses. As I felt myself yielding to sleep, I felt sickened and wondered if he had any idea of how his son was swindling him.

And with Guiseppi no longer in the frame, would Selene now be back with Justin in Five Oaks Manor?

Chapter 14

I woke up fully energised the following morning. With much of the mystery now solved, I had a number of new options to consider. Already, I had decided to walk away from my goddess – and failed. Now, with even more reason to do so, I should renew my efforts with greater determination.

But I still only had Guiseppi's word that Selene was alive and well. On the face of it, he had fed me a useful clue, but that could be all part of his cover-up strategy – muddying the waters. As I had already decided, the only way I could be sure was to see her myself. And then again, my passion for the girl was undiminished. It was impossible to deny, even to myself, that I desperately wanted to see her again. I could not rid myself of my obsession without some sort of resolution.

But all that would have to wait. I had several property viewings arranged for today, although I was now having second thoughts about renting a place. I had seen only one that I felt comfortable in, and it was very expensive. I had my little house in Italy and could afford to relax for the moment, to take time to find a more permanent home – perhaps to buy. But I still had to sort out some storage space.

I had planned to return to Norfolk the following day, but things had changed and instead, I would spend the day in Sussex.

The heat and humidity had been building, and it was sweltering as I drove south. It was mid-morning by the time I pulled up in front of the Courtney family house, and once again winced as the electronic chimes announced my arrival. In such a large house, it can take some time to answer the door, and I waited patiently for it to be opened – but by whom, I wondered. If it wasn't to be Justin, I was half expecting Selene herself to appear. But when it did eventually open, I was surprised to find myself faced with a complete stranger.

He was a slim, good-looking man with fair ginger hair, complete with associated freckles that were generously sprinkled over his nose and cheeks. As he smiled his welcome, he reminded me of a model from the pages of a mail-order clothing catalogue demonstrating how happy you would feel if you were to purchase the flower-patterned shirt he was wearing.

"Hi," he greeted me. "How can I help you?"

"Hi. I wanted a word with Justin. I was in the area and thought I'd call in."

"He's out, I'm afraid." He looked briefly at his watch. "But ... he shouldn't be long now. Do you want to wait for him?" Without waiting for a reply, he opened the door wider and backed up against it saying, "Do come in."

As we crossed the hall to the large kitchen he offered, "Can I make you a coffee? Or maybe you'd like a cold drink – some apple juice perhaps? It's really hot now, isn't it?"

"It is," I agreed. "I've been in the car for more than a couple of hours. I'd just love some of that apple juice." He made for the fridge, pointing me to a seat in the bay window.

"I'm Larry, by the way," he said, as he poured me a glass and set it down on the table in front of me.

I shook the hand he offered. "Martin," I said.

Larry settled back in his chair before asking, "So, how do you know Justin?"

I had mentally prepared opening remarks depending on whether it was Justin or Selene who answered the door, but this question from the young man was off my script.

"To be honest, I've only met him a couple of times," I answered rather lamely. "I was after some information about a property owned by his father."

"Right. Well, he should be able to help you. He deals with all his father's affairs. His father's in a home, you know."

"Yes. I know. I visited him there. I caused an outburst – embarrassing!"

"Oh, I believe I heard about it. Well, it happens, I know. Poor chap." After a couple of seconds, he continued, "It's a good home though. It should be – it costs enough."

"I'm sure," I said and paused, uncertain how to continue.

Eventually, I dived straight in, "I know Justin's out, but is Selene in perhaps?"

"*Selene?*" He almost shouted it, and then laughed. "Selene," he repeated. "You mean Robertson's wife?"

"Yes," I said, surprised at his reaction. "I thought she lived here with Justin."

Larry threw back his head with laughter. "Where the hell did you get that idea?"

My theory was rapidly collapsing. "I don't know," was all I could muster. "I just put a few bits of information together ... and I seem to have come up with the wrong answer."

"You certainly have. Do you know where she is?"

This question drove another nail in the coffin of my theory. If Justin didn't know where she was, then I was back to square one. "No. That's exactly what I'm trying to find out. I thought she was at least a friend of Justin – and that he'd know where she was."

"*A friend of Justin?* You must be joking. He hates her. He blames her for his father's condition."

"Oh, I doubt that," I said.

"I know. It's unlikely. But he believes it – that's the point. And she certainly can't have helped. She likes to hurt men."

I groaned inside. Not more advice to stay clear of her, I thought. I simply frowned, but he must have noticed. "Well," he continued, "she's damaged goods. Something in the past – her stepfather probably."

"She mentioned him," I agreed. "She doesn't like him very much."

"I know. I think her father was Greek – killed in some sort of boating accident when she was a baby. I don't know much about her wretched stepfather, only what I read in the papers. I think Justin has met him though, and I know he has all sorts of suspicions, including domestic abuse. But it's all second-hand stuff, and I probably shouldn't be saying anything."

"Well, if there's any truth in it, she's had quite a lot to contend with in her life. After him, she was physically damaged by her first husband."

"How do you mean?" Larry demanded, frowning.

"In a car crash. He was drunk apparently. She lost the use of her legs ..."

"Is that what she told you?" He interrupted. "You don't want to believe much of what she says – if anything at all." He shook his head. "It wasn't Seb who was driving, and it was she who had been drinking far too much. Poor old Sebastian died. I knew him well ... he was a lovely young chap."

He paused, remembering his friend, and then added, "She was so lucky not to have ended up in prison. She's got Robertson to thank for that."

It was my turn to ask, "What do you mean?"

"Robertson was a noted surgeon, and he moved in society circles. He had fallen for her during all the months he had spent operating on her and supervising her recovery. When she didn't have the money, he engaged one of the county's leading barristers to mastermind her defence. He was brilliant apparently, and got her off with just a fine and a suspended sentence."

"So that's where they met. He was her surgeon."

"That's right. Like many before and after, he was smitten." He paused then and seemed to study me intently. Then he asked with a grin on his face, "Are you one of her admirers, Martin?"

I felt myself blushing. "Well, I only met her once, but I certainly found her fascinating."

Larry continued to smile knowingly and nodded his head several times. "Be careful, Martin."

Yet another warning! I was wearying of them.

"Has she been here at the house recently?" I asked, changing the subject.

"Not for several months – probably a year or more in fact."

"I asked because I thought I saw her at the window when I was here last. Justin said it was your cleaner, a Mrs Greatorix if I remember right."

Larry gave a short laugh. "Does nobody tell the truth?" He exclaimed. "Mrs Greatorix hasn't been here since Robertson went into the home a couple of years ago. It was probably me at the window. I like to keep tabs on any man who visits Justin. Actually, I think I remember seeing you now."

So that was it. My theory was totally in tatters. Larry was looking at me quizzically.

"You don't get it, do you?" he said. "Justin and I are gay. We live here together. Selene simply wouldn't be welcome," he joked. "We look after the house and Justin manages all Robertson's financial affairs. He looks after the inside of the house, and I keep the gardens. We usually cook together."

"So neither of you go out to work?" I asked.

"No. It all takes quite a bit of time, you know. It's a big house, and the gardens are extensive. Anyway, we're both writers. We each have a novel on the go, and we work together writing series for TV. We tried sitcoms, but they didn't work out too well. I think our dramas will do better. I hope so, anyway."

So there it was. I was wrong even there. It appeared they were not cheating Justin's father as I had thought. Larry lifted his head and looked out of the window as we heard the sound of a car's wheels rolling over the gravel drive. Justin must have parked in the rear garages, as I heard him enter through the back door in the kitchen lobby.

"Hi, Smooch," he shouted. "I'm back."

His face was a picture as he came into the room. Larry looked at me, smiled, and shrugged. "It's something to do with the way I dance," he explained away his nickname.

Justin sprang back to life. "I'm sorry. I didn't know you had company." He looked at me, and then said, "It's Martin isn't it?"

"Yes. Hi, Justin. I was in the area and thought I'd look you up."

I could see he was finding this a bit weird, so I continued quickly, "I wanted to thank you for the tip you gave me when I was here last. I went out to Italy and tracked down Selene's Italian friend."

This impressed him, and he yelped incredulously, "Barone Morandi? You went to Italy to see him?"

"Well ... Yes. But I have a house out there – not far from the house on the lake. It's only a few hours away from the Morandi estate."

This seemed to settle Justin, and I continued, "I had to find out what had happened out there, and I got the story from him."

Justin wandered over to the fridge and pulled out an open bottle of white wine. "I'd be interested to hear it," he said, as he poured three glasses. We sat around the table and I gave them a full account of the circumstances leading up to Guiseppi's wounding. Justin and Larry listened in silence, taking the occasional sip of wine.

When I had finished, Larry spoke first, "So ... Selene strikes again."

Justin said nothing, but pursed his lips and nodded.

I said, "Of course, we've only got Guiseppi's word for it. None of this proves that she's alive. And if she is – where she is."

There was a moment's silence before Justin spoke quietly into the table, "She is alive. I don't know where she is right now, but I know where she'll be next week."

I looked at him, speechless. Larry joined me, both of us silently demanding that he continue.

Justin looked up and smiled at our two expectant faces, "She telephoned the other day. She was planning a trip – wanted some money."

"I suppose you arranged it for her?" I questioned.

"Yes, of course. Why do you ask?"

I shrugged. "Larry says you dislike her."

He looked disapprovingly at Larry. "Did he just?"

It was Larry's turn to shrug. "I was just explaining the situation. She had fed Martin a whole load of lies."

"Well, she's not my favourite person, I have to admit. But she is my father's wife, and he still loves her. I promised him I would let her have whatever she needs, and he has the funds. In fact, she's not too demanding."

"You say you know where she'll be next week?" I queried.

"Isle of Wight," he said. "It's Cowes week."

"Do you know where she'll be staying? Did you reserve a hotel room?"

"No, I don't. And no, I didn't." Justin looked at me sternly. "For Goodness' sake, Martin – you're not still chasing her?"

The two men sat looking at me, and I felt embarrassed once again. "I just want to see her again – to be sure she is safe and well," I insisted. "That's all. I've spent several weeks on it now, and I want to see it through."

Justin smiled. "OK," he said. "I believe you. Just be careful, Martin. She both loves men and hates them. She traps them and spits them out. It's happened time and time again."

"Et tu, Brute?" I smiled ruefully. "Larry's already warned me. I think I've had enough advice on the subject."

"Well, take it seriously. Just ask Guiseppi Morandi." I didn't tell them that the Barone had already issued his own stern warnings.

Mercifully, they offered no more advice as I thanked them both for their help and said my goodbyes. I felt quite elated as I drove back to my hotel. The end of my search seemed to be no more than a week away.

Chapter 15

It was time for a decision. Once again, my mind told me to return to my father in Norfolk, see the divorce through to its end, and get on with my life. But my heart still told me otherwise.

All the negative advice and dire warnings I had received over the last few days seemed perversely to have deepened my obsession with Selene. Right from the start, I had found her highly fanciable. Add to that fascinating and flirtatious. Now a frisson of fear had been added to the mix and I knew, well before I was halfway back to my hotel, that I would be taking a ferry to the Isle of Wight at some point during the coming week.

I decided to spend one last night in the area and called at the house to pick up another batch of clothes to add to the sad pile of belongings that littered my hotel room. Angie came in from work while I was there and, for old times' sake, we decided to go out to dinner at the local curry house. I don't know whether the grapevine had penetrated this establishment or whether it was simply our lack of appearance over recent weeks, but the staff was extremely welcoming and solicitous. It made for a very odd evening, so similar to those many others we had enjoyed over the last ten years, and yet so different – very probably our last meal together.

We chose our usual dishes and ordered our usual drinks. For the most part, even our conversation pursued familiar lines. I was approaching the bottom of my second glass of lager before she asked me what I had been doing. She already knew I had moved in with my father, but that would only occupy a portion of my time so I had to give her a brief account of my efforts to find Selene. She was intrigued and questioned me closely.

"Why the hell didn't you tell me about it before?" She demanded. I shrugged, more relaxed than I felt. Where was this going?

"I don't know. The chance never came up somehow – things being as they were. Events just overtook us."

"Come on, Martin. You could have found the time when you got back from Italy. What was your relationship with this girl – Selene? Did you sleep with her?"

"No, no. Nothing like that – I never even kissed her. It was just one small meeting, an afternoon in the sun. That's all."

"*That's all?*" She mimicked. "There has to be more to it than that. You don't go chasing her around the world for nothing."

"I've already explained. Something happened to her. The police gave up and I had to find out if she survived – whether she was alive or dead." I paused briefly, and then added, "I have the time, and I quite enjoy the detective work."

Angie remained silent as I continued, "Anyway, I seem to have found her now, and she sounds to be OK."

"So that's it then. Case closed," said Angie.

"Probably," I accepted, hedging my bets.

"Hmm," she muttered, apparently agreeing to close the subject unresolved.

We continued to chat over another drink and then coffee, and only left when it was clear they wished to close up. We parted as friends, and I was pleased that the subject had finally been aired in a manner that was unlikely to affect the agreed divorce arrangements.

The following day, I loaded up the car with files, clothes, CDs, and a couple of large boxes of miscellaneous items, and headed for Norfolk.

I sank into the cocoon of life in my father's house. I was aware that such comfort would not suit me for long, but it was appropriate for me right then – for a few days at least. It gave me time to consider my next move. I had been hesitant in my conversation with Angie, but I was secretly certain that I would follow through with my plan and attempt to meet up with Selene in Cowes.

But I had to think it through. What was the worst that could happen? She may have hooked up with another man. Even if not, she may want nothing to do with me and cut me dead. Either way, it would mark an end to my obsession. At least I would then be able to get on with life, content in the knowledge that she was safe.

But first, I had to meet up with her. Justin had made no reservation for her, so either she had made her own arrangements or she was accompanying someone. She may not be easy to find, and I needed a plan. I would be unlikely to stray far from the town of Cowes, so decided that a car would be unnecessary. Getting there would be easy enough, and a few clicks secured me e-tickets for a fast passenger crossing, along with nearby parking in Southampton. Accommodation during Cowes Week proved far more difficult and expensive, however, and it was nearly an hour before I managed to secure a small single room in a B & B some five minutes from the town centre.

I was aware that Selene moved in circles unfamiliar to me, and probably way above my pay grade. I decided to search the internet for the sort of accommodation she might frequent, and for functions she would be likely to attend. The town did not appear to be blessed with many luxury hotels, with some of the best reviewed being converted houses. I began to think she would perhaps be more likely to rent an apartment for the week.

Cowes is not a large town, but she was going to be difficult to find in the festival crowd. As a teenager, many years earlier, I had enjoyed a day trip to the island, but all I could recall was a train that ran the length of the pier and a large sandy beach – nothing that was going to be of any use in my search. And I knew almost nothing about sailing, which would severely limit my conversation. I was aware that a sheet was not something you slept under, and that a boom was not just a noise, but a spar of wood attached to the sheet that hit you and hurt your head. I knew a few other words, like clew, fid and gaff, but had no idea what they were or how to use them.

The Royal Yacht Squadron had an internet site and was clearly at the epicentre of Cowes during race week. Housed in the old Castle, a canon on its waterfront promenade is fired to start every race. Much of the after-race entertainment also takes place in this august establishment, and I decided that this was probably where I would find Selene – at the heart of everything.

But as I read on, it became clear that to meet up with her there would be extremely difficult, if not impossible. The Squadron is one of the most prestigious yacht clubs in the world, with restricted and highly exclusive membership. Only members are permitted through its hallowed portals, and only recently, the Queen herself was refused entrance through its front doors and had to be smuggled in through a side annexe. Queen Victoria was completely denied access into the Castle. What chance had I?

The fine spell had broken by the time I had parked the car, and I had to negotiate the five-minute walk to the terminal in light rain. The wind was getting up and the gangway was heaving as I boarded the ferry. It was crowded on board and I squatted on my case at the end of a row of seats. The rain was falling harder now, and I watched the droplets meander slowly down the window by my side as we waited for the half-hour journey to start. It was going to be a lumpy crossing.

On my other side, a woman was busy with a biro and a book of puzzles. I had completed the occasional crossword and Sudoku puzzle, but this was different. It resembled a cross between the two, but with hexagonal boxes, instead of square. And she was filling them in with letters, rather than numbers.

"What do you have to do with that?" I asked looking at the puzzle after we had been going for a while.

"Find words, in all directions," she explained briefly, looking up at me. She was much younger than I had expected, maybe even younger than me, but the quick view of her suggested a rather plain face. Against the elements, she was wearing a voluminous red anorak, with the hood still pulled over her head so that I was unable to see much of her.

"Hmm, looks a bit too difficult for me," I said.

"No. It's just a question of familiarity – getting into the mind of the person who constructs them."

"Hmm," I mused again, sceptical. "Are you racing at Cowes?"

"Good Lord no," she exclaimed, laughing. "I don't go on boats unless I have to – like today. I'm a terrible sailor. I get sick on the Serpentine."

"You're doing OK today. It's turned pretty rough."

"Well, I don't feel too great, I warn you," she said with a smile. "I'll try to give you a few seconds' warning, and then you'd better be ready to move pretty damn fast."

"If you're not going for the sailing, what are you doing on board? Do you live on the island?"

"No." She paused, looking at me. "I'm going to meet a chap who's there for the sailing."

Maybe she thought she had disappointed me, for she added quickly, "We were engaged to be married, but I called it off. I'm not sure ..." she tailed off, collecting her thoughts. "I suppose this trip is to make my mind up – one way or the other. I'm not looking forward to it."

"Take your time. It's best to be sure. My marriage has cracked up." As I said it, I almost bit my tongue. Wasn't it far too early to talk of such things? But she had been so open about her problems, it just seemed to be a natural progression, so I continued lamely, "The divorce is nearly through."

"I'm sorry," she said. "It's a rotten time. My brother went through it, so I know how hard it is."

"Yup," I shrugged. "It happens." There was a short lull in the conversation when I decided not to take the topic any further.

"Are you a sailor then?" she asked, reopening the conversation.

"No. I steer well clear of boats too. I did sail once – in a flooded quarry. Every time we tacked, a lump of wood hit me on the back of the head. It wasn't very successful."

"So what are you doing here then?"

"It's a long story. I don't have time for it all now, but I'll be trying to find someone I met briefly a couple of months ago. When I went to see them again at the same place, the house had been broken into and trashed, with loads of blood everywhere. The police washed their hands of it, and I've spent my time trying to find out what happened. I think I should have been a detective – I've enjoyed it."

"How fascinating. So, how far have you got?"

"I hope I'm nearly finished. She's supposed to be in Cowes this week. All I've got to do is find her ..."

"Aha!" she exclaimed. "It's a girl you're chasing, eh?"

"No," I insisted loudly and then added, as if to confirm that I had no interest in her, "She's a paraplegic – in a wheelchair."

"Oh. What a story. I'd love to be there at the end."

I waved a hand helplessly in the air. "Goodness knows when that will be. I haven't a clue how I'm going to find her. She moves in very different circles from me. Even if I find out where she is, I'm not sure if I'll be able to meet up with her."

The catamaran was about to dock, and the passengers began swarming towards the gangway. "I'll keep an eye out for her," she called after me as we shuffled forward. She used either her feminine wiles or more brute force than me, but she was soon five or six persons ahead as we filed slowly through the exit corridor. I didn't expect to see her again, but as I left the terminal and turned into the High Street, she was there waiting for me. It was still raining, and her hood covered all but a smiling face.

"Do you have time for a cup of tea?" I suggested.

She raised her wrist and looked at her watch, as does anyone when asked such a question.

"I don't see why not," she said. "Brad will be out on the water somewhere no doubt."

"What, in this?" I questioned, gesticulating about the weather.

"Oh, this is nothing. They go out in just about anything."

We pushed on along the High Street, which was a solid mass of humanity with people bumping into each other as they kept their heads down against the rain. We passed by a couple of modern coffee shops where clients were standing in queues to be served. Ducking into a quieter side street, we came across an old-fashioned cafe offering cream teas – just what I was after. It too was busy, but we were in luck as a couple were just leaving, and we thankfully took their vacated table before anyone else could get to it.

As I sat down opposite my new friend I said, "It's ridiculous. I know the name of your ex-fiancé, but I don't know yours. Mine's Martin." I offered my hand, and found myself saying rather awkwardly, "I assume that handshakes are in order."

She smiled, took my hand and responded, "I can't think of anything more appropriate. Mine's Julie."

She had taken off her anorak and hung it over the back of her chair. Sitting opposite, I now had a head-on view of her and was surprisingly impressed. Julie was no classic beauty – many people would not even find her pretty. Her slightly humped nose and large round brown eyes gave her a somewhat owl-like appearance. And there was something new – something I hadn't spotted on the boat. When she blinked, her left eyelid reopened slightly slower than the right. I believe some people refer to it as a lazy eye, but I had never come across it before. It added further interest to a face that was already full of character, and I found it attractive.

"You said you would look out for Selene," I started. "That would be great. I think we could be of use to one another here. We both have a tricky job to do. You might need a shoulder to cry on, and I could certainly do with help. What do you think? Shouldn't we keep in touch?"

She gave me a long, searching stare before agreeing, "Yes. Why not – it's probably a good idea."

I dug into a pocket for my phone. "Let's swap numbers before we forget."

We had just finished this, when a somewhat harassed waitress appeared at our table and took our order for cream teas, seemingly the universal choice in the room.

As we talked, we each mentally sketched a picture of the other. It followed the usual pattern that people use on first acquaintance – where they were born, where they live now, how they make a living, and how they like to spend their spare time. Julie was working her way to becoming an account manager in a leading advertising agency in Baker Street. Raised in Surrey's stockbroker belt, for the last couple of years she had shared a flat with two other girls in the Kensington/Earl's Court area, and it was there that she had met Brad.

The three girls were spending the evening in their favourite local bar, eating and drinking at the expense of Alicia, a model who had just landed a lucrative assignment in Paris. A group of Australian men were noisily enjoying a raucous time, totally dominating the bar area. Towards the end of the evening, three of them detached themselves and came over to join the girls at their table. One of them stood out from the others – a real hunk of Aussie manhood. Julie had always considered her two friends to be far more attractive than herself, and she was surprised when he chose to sit down beside her. She was even more amazed later outside their flat when the girls having turned down the boys' suggestions of "coming up for a coffee", he asked for her telephone number. Their romance flourished quickly. Far from being the coarse, macho Antipodean she had first imagined, he was kind, well-mannered and attentive – even a trifle shy.

On the first anniversary of their meeting, he surprised her once again. They had gone for a stroll in the local park when Brad suddenly endangered the sharp creases in his trousers by ducking down on one knee, taking hold of her hand, and pulling a ring from his pocket. Her first reaction was to laugh out loud, but she soon stopped when she realised that he was serious. It was such a shock, she was unable to give him an answer that evening but, after a night's deliberation, she turned over to wake him up with a kiss and a "Yes".

But over the next several months, cracks in their relationship began to appear and Julie realised why she had been reticent on that day. Their temperaments appeared to complement each other. Despite his shyness, he was more of an extrovert – forever partying and always seeking out the action. Normally this worked well, but did occasionally lead to some friction. Also, Brad often spoke nostalgically about home, and she anticipated that he would someday wish to return to Oz. She didn't fancy that one bit.

However, their wildly different interests were the root of more serious problems. Whilst Julie loved the theatre, art and books, he was more of an action man and, in common with many Australian men, was fanatical about sports of all kinds. In particular, his great obsession was sailing and, with the winter months over, he began spending all his leisure hours on the water. She accompanied him at first but, although she was a strong swimmer, the movement of small boats upset her stomach. This was exacerbated by the role of chef, cleaner and general dogsbody that the crew normally assigned to her, and it was not long before she stayed at home.

As spring morphed imperceptibly into summer, she found herself alone much of the time. She tackled him about it one evening. He appeared to be understanding but could offer no solution. "It's my life, Jules. You can't ask me to give it up. You really can't ..."

Julie shrugged, but she had already made up her mind and handed the ring back to Brad – gently, kindly, with tears in her eyes and apologies on her lips. "I'm so sorry Brad. I can't see it working though. Our interests are way too far apart. We'd never last the distance."

"And that's where we are now," she said, as she finished her potted history of life with Brad. "He begged me to come out here for Cowes Week – said there'd be lots of entertainment that I'd like. I doubt that, and I'm dreading the place he'll have arranged for us to stay. It'll be some god-awful shack, shared with a whole load of other sailors. It'll stink of sweat and unwashed socks. I don't think I'll be changing my mind, but I feel that I owe him the time."

More than an hour had flown by, and she got up. "We really ought to let someone have our table." I looked around and realised that I hadn't noticed how busy the place still was.

Outside, the rain had eased and we stood looking at each other, unsure of what to do or say. I was tempted to kiss her on the cheek to say goodbye. We had exchanged intimacies, and I had the feeling she might expect it. It was touch and go for a second or two but eventually, I simply said, "Well, I hope to see you during the week then, Julie."

"Yes," she said. "I'm sure we'll meet up somewhere. Good luck with your search."

"And you," I replied, as we both turned to walk in opposite directions.

Chapter 16

I dug out the little map I had printed. My room turned out to be in the midst of bungalow land and consisted of a box room into which a bed had been squeezed to take advantage of the exceptional call for accommodation during this special week. But at least it was a bed and only about ten minutes from where the action was. The owner, a trim figure in her mid-fifties, had the good grace to offer apologies for its size, but I waved them aside, wishing to keep her on my side.

"You must have seen many Cowes Weeks," I suggested.

"A few," she said with a smile.

"This is only my second visit to the island – a long time ago. I remember a long pier with a railway on it."

"Ah, that'll be Ryde," she explained. "Ryde is for holidays. Cowes is for sport."

"How long have you been here?"

"Ouf, more than thirty years now."

"You sail?"

"I used to. Don't do much these days. My husband still sails though. He's part owner of a Sonar."

"Sorry. That means nothing to me," I said. Once again, I wondered how I was to hold a conversation in the company of real sailors.

"It's a class of yacht. They race them here." She smiled, immediately realising that I was no seadog. "It's a funny time to visit Cowes if you're not here for the racing."

"I suppose so," I agreed. "I'm looking for someone – a girl."

"Aha," she winked. "I'm afraid it's a very small bed."

I think I probably blushed a little. "No. No. It's not like that. I've been worried about her safety. I just want to make sure she's alright."

"Aha," was her only comment.

"The trouble is, I don't know where she's staying. She has money, and she's used to the high life. Have you any idea where she might stay?"

She thought for a few seconds and then said, "Not easy. There are some nice small hotels, but none you'd call international. The yacht clubs have rooms for their members. I'll have a chat with my husband when he comes in. He may have some ideas, and I'll make a list of places you could try."

"That would be good. Many thanks."

I unpacked what I could into the small chest of drawers, and hung up my best trousers and a suit on a hook on the back of the door. With nothing more I could achieve, I removed my shoes and lay down on the bed to read the thriller I had packed for such moments. But it failed to thrill to the extent suggested by the cover picture, and it was not long before the book fell listlessly onto my lap, and my mind turned to thoughts of Selene, and my conversation that afternoon with Julie.

Oddly, meeting Julie seemed to have caused a subtle twist to my longing for Selene. Suddenly, my quest seemed slightly less urgent, less all-consuming. There was no question of her wresting my heart away from Selene. She was a very pleasant girl, perfectly presentable, but I felt little of the sheer animal attraction that radiated so brilliantly from Selene. I suppose, in some way, she may have lessened the tension. Perhaps, after all, it would not be such a catastrophe if I failed to land my quarry. Julie had validated the old expression that I had somehow forgotten but seemed so appropriate here in Cowes, *there are plenty more fish in the sea*.

A knock on the door interrupted my thoughts and Joan, as the owner had introduced herself, entered the room. A frown immediately clouded her face, but it disappeared as soon as she saw that my shoes were off my feet and on the floor.

"Here's the list I promised you," she said. "Jim's included three or four hotels and some of the major clubs. He's noted them down on this little street map. You know you won't be able to get into the Castle if she has that sort of influence. The Squadron doesn't allow anyone in who's not a member."

"Yes," I replied. "I read all about it online. I don't know whether she knows anyone like that."

"Well. Good luck," she smiled as she left.

The first hotel on Jim's list turned out to be only a couple of hundred yards down the road towards the sea. As I entered, the reception desk was unmanned, and I walked past it into a lounge which then opened out into a bar area. The barman made no effort to check my status as a resident and happily pulled me a very welcome pint, which I took over to an inconspicuous table in the corner. There was only one elderly couple in the room, slowly sipping their glasses of wine, and I pulled out my book to await events.

I had timed it well and within less than half an hour, the sailing community began to arrive in groups of varying sizes, all gradually joining up to form a noisy throng around the bar. By the time I had finished my pint, there was no sign of Selene and I decided it was time to move on. I was feeling rather perplexed as I mounted the steps to the next hotel. If I continued along the same lines, I was destined to be drunk long before I met up with Selene. I needed a new strategy. There had to be a better way. Again, no one challenged me as I entered the hotel, but I turned to the attractive young receptionist.

"I'm trying to meet up with someone. Is it alright if I check if she's in the bar?"

"No problem," she agreed immediately. That'll save both time and my liver, I thought.

But Selene did not show up. Neither did she appear at any of the other hotels that night. I did have some success at the last – not with my search for Selene, but with an excellent dinner, which allowed me to return to my tiny hovel in rather better spirits than might be expected.

I did not sleep well, however. I don't believe I had considered just how frustrating a business this was going to be. But the night's thoughts failed to come up with any hopeful shortcut, and I set off to the sea front after an excellent breakfast, large enough to last me until dinner. I spent the day at several locations, alternately looking out for a wheelchair and trying to make some sort of sense of the yacht races. I cannot claim success in either activity, but the weather had taken a change for the better and I spent a pleasant enough day in the sun.

In the evening, I set off to check out the sailing clubs promising myself that, at some point in the evening, I would place my stomach in the safe hands of the previous night's chef. Leaving until last any club with "Royal" in its name, I was surprised to be challenged as I entered the first. I have no idea whether he knew all the club members, but the man on the door certainly recognised that I was not one of them.

"I'm sorry," I had rehearsed my response. "I hope I'm in the right place. Sir John suggested I should meet him here. Do you mind if I look around for him?"

"Sir John who?" he queried.

"Ah," I stumbled. "I can't recall. I only met him the other day."

"Would it be Sir John Halland?"

"Ah, yes. That was it."

"I'm sorry. He's not in." He paused. "I don't believe he's a member." And he paused once again before delivering the coup de grace, "In fact, I've never heard of him."

He had caught me out. "I'm sorry," I said. "I must have made a mistake," and left with my tail firmly between my legs.

I was able to gain a brief look inside a couple of the other clubs, but with no sign of Selene, I was losing heart rapidly. Over another excellent dinner, I started wondering whether she was in Cowes at all. Was Justin misinforming me again? Why would he? It was a disappointing day, but my luck was about to turn.

After breakfast the following morning, I was just leaving the house when my mobile rang. It was Julie.

"Good morning, Martin. How's your hide and seek coming on?"

"Hi, Julie. Not very well, I'm afraid. Bloody terribly in fact. I'm not getting anywhere, and I'm bored with it now."

"Well, I've got some news that may cheer you up. I told Brad about your little adventure, and he said last night that he thinks he saw her – a very pretty blond girl in a wheelchair."

She couldn't see how my eyes lit up, but she must certainly have noticed the excitement in my voice.

"Great! That certainly sounds like her. Where did he see her? Did he say?"

"On the front – near the starting gun. She was with a group of people, and one of them Brad recognised – the press baron, Sir James Marshall. You've heard of him?"

"Yes, of course. He's often on TV. I can't say I've ever taken to him though. Now I dislike him even more."

"Brad says it was quite a big group of people. Your girl may be nothing to do with him."

"I hope not."

"Anyway, they will almost certainly be going to the big dinner tomorrow night. It's a sort of end-of-Cowes Week celebration for all the sailors. And even better news – I've got you a ticket."

"Oh Julie, that's fantastic – so good of you."

"Brad got it. Thank him when you see him. It'll cost you £50, but that includes wine with the meal. Then there's a cash bar for everything else. Is that OK?"

"That's wonderful," I said excitedly. "It's made my day."

"It's in the Pavilion. That's in the grounds of the Castle – the only part of the Royal Yacht Squadron open to non-members. It should be great."

"I've read about the Pavilion. Have you any idea what I should wear?"

"Er ... No. I'll ask Brad. Anyway, I have your ticket here, and I ought to get it to you beforehand, so we don't have to hang around outside. What are you doing today?"

"I've got nothing in particular planned. I expect I'll go down to the front and look out for this Marshall group. What about lunch – if you're free?"

"Brad will be out in the boat, so that would be nice – yes."

"My landlady gives me a really good breakfast, so I don't eat much at midday. How about meeting in the place we know – the teashop. They'll do some sort of light snacks. Is twelve-thirty OK?"

"That's fine. I'll see you there."

My search for Selene had suddenly lost much of its impetus. With the apparent certainty of meeting up with her the next day, all the urgency had evaporated. I did wander down to the front to watch the races and believe that I did even catch a distant glimpse of her on the Castle's lawns. But any thoughts of how to follow it up played a secondary role in the anticipation I was feeling for my lunch with Julie.

She was late, and I had been sitting by myself at our table for nearly a quarter of an hour when my phone warbled.

"There's been an incident in one of the races," Julie explained. "Brad's not involved, but I had to make sure. "I'll be there in five minutes. Sorry."

Good as her word, it was almost exactly five minutes later that she sat down opposite me at the same table we had occupied a couple of days earlier. A huge smile spread across her face, probably caused by the coup she had achieved on my behalf, but I chose to believe it was the pleasure of seeing me again.

"Any luck?" she asked.

I shook my head. "The only luck I've had on this island is meeting you."

"Smoothie," she accused, but with another smile.

"No. I'm serious. If I hadn't hooked up with you, I'd be in a right mess by now – no contact, and no prospect of any. I'm greatly indebted.

"Good," she said, as she pulled a formal gold-edged invitation card out of her purse and handed it to me. I took out my wallet and exchanged it for £50 in notes.

"What was the problem?" I asked.

"Oh, a couple of boats collided when they rounded a buoy. It happens sometimes. They're all very competitive. Nobody was hurt though, as I understand it."

"So, are you enjoying the races?" I asked. "I've watched a number, but I can't understand what's going on."

"No. It's not easy. Skips often use their skills to take very different courses. The only time you can see who's leading is when they round the buoy at the end of each leg. It's easier when you watch on television with computer graphics to help."

"I've never watched it. I find it all very confusing. How's Brad doing?"

"Not bad. Overall, he's running about fifth in class. He's quite happy with that."

We chatted over quiches and coffee for an hour or so before returning to the quay, where Julie made one last effort to implant into me the mysteries of yacht racing. She failed, but we enjoyed each other's company and I went to bed that night feeling oddly composed. I would undoubtedly be nervous tomorrow evening as my hunt staggered to its conclusion. But whatever happened as I finally met up with Selene, it might not be the end of my world. Julie had shown me that. I was not looking at her as some sort of reserve, but perhaps in my all-consuming infatuation with Selene, I had been carried away by unreasoned passion. Julie's friendship had brought some balancing sense into it – and reminded me that there was another big world out there.

Chapter 17

The sun decided to shine majestically on my big day – one of those glorious summer days that reminds one of one's youth. And it was as a schoolboy that I spent the entire day, like the last day of term, with nothing much to do, marking time and waiting impatiently, full of anticipation.

Brad had suggested that the evening would be a reasonably informal affair. He would be in slacks and a blazer, but he thought that others might be wearing something more formal. Fortunately, I'd had the foresight to pack a suit, but in the holiday atmosphere of the island, I felt rather conspicuous as I walked down towards the Castle.

The Pavilion was already buzzing when I arrived, everyone crowding around the bar. It would be impossible to get a drink yet, so I started on a quick tour. Tables set for dinner occupied most of the main room, and they even extended into the covered terrace that looked out over the lawns that lead down to the sea wall.

As I turned back towards the bar, I spotted Julie. If my eyes had lighted on her earlier, I hadn't recognised her. Her face wore only a mere hint of makeup and her trim body was clothed in a gaily-coloured summer dress. She looked splendid. It was easy to distinguish Brad as he stood beside her, a tall athletically built man with a handsome weather-beaten face beneath a mop of wavy golden hair. Standing together, the two looked to be an ideal partnership. What a pity, I thought, that such a picture-perfect couple seemed destined to drift apart.

But the thought passed rapidly as I experienced a slight thrill somewhere deep inside of me – somewhere around the region of my gut, one I had experienced a hundred times before. If the liaison was doomed to failure, she perhaps could be mine. But what was this? I was just about to meet up with Selene – the woman who had inhabited all of my dreams over the last several months. Did I have to possess every woman? What was wrong with me? Was I different from other men?

Julie smiled as I approached, and touched Brad's arm to get his attention.

"Hi, Martin," she greeted me. "This is Brad. Brad ... Martin."

"Hi Martin," the big man echoed, taking my outstretched hand into his enormous palm. "I've heard a lot about you."

He introduced me to the others in his party. Geoff and Frazer made up the rest of his crew and Shirley was Frazer's girlfriend. The men were all dressed alike in blue blazers, red trousers and boat shoes, and once more made me feel somewhat overdressed. If this made me feel slightly awkward, what followed made me positively embarrassed, and I felt my face begin to flush.

"Martin has been chasing a girl around the world," Brad announced, "and he hopes to meet up with her – *here – tonight* ..." I began to counter their laughter with protestations that it was all lies, but stopped almost immediately when I realised it was nothing more than the truth. Why should I deny it? I joined in with their laughter.

They were a pleasant, lively group, full of jokes and banter about the day's racing. Much of this was over my head, but they went out of their way to make me feel welcome. After a quarter of an hour or so, Julie tugged at my sleeve saying, "I think your girl's party has arrived." I turned to look towards the other end of the bar and immediately recognised the press baron.

No one could miss or fail to recognise such a man. He was huge – in all directions. A dark five o'clock shadow covered most of his otherwise ruddy face from which jet-black hair was swept back and over his forehead with no visible parting. This gave him an unfortunate, slightly satanic appearance – such that many people took an instant dislike to him even before he opened his mouth. And when he did speak, he would invariably manage to alienate still more. And I was one of them.

He was dressed like Brad and his friends in red trousers and a blue jacket that sported an elaborate gold and red badge on the breast pocket. It all looked rather incongruous on his portly frame.

Anyone failing to recognise the man from his appearance would do so from his voice – one heard frequently on the radio. I was suddenly aware that I could hear it above the already loud background hubbub of hundreds of simultaneous conversations. It was a voice that started way down deep within his body, amplified as it passed through his barrel chest, and finally sharpened with its distinctive rasp as it emerged through his throat to his mouth.

I could see no women in the group that surrounded him. It seemed to consist entirely of men ranging from rosy-cheeked youths to silver-haired elders, all eagerly looking up at the big man, apparently hanging on his every word of wisdom.

Both Julie and I were effectively side-lined by the main topic of conversation in our group, and she happily agreed to my suggestion that we should take a wander towards the group to see if we could spot any sign of Selene. I could feel my nervousness rising as we approached, my heart rate increasing. Then it suddenly took a leap forward as a gap appeared and we got our first glimpse of Selene in her wheelchair. She was parked immediately beside Marshall, looking up at him and smiling. I was amazed and not a little disappointed. What was she to him? What was he to her?

But, as I stared at her face, it was just as I had remembered it. In daydreams and at night, I had seen it a hundred times over the last few months. And I had recalled it well. All at once, my purpose renewed and strengthened, her status as my goddess was reinstated, and I could think of nothing more than the need to make her my own.

I stood still, watching her for several moments. I felt my mouth hanging slightly open and closed it only when I felt Julie watching me. I briefly turned to look at her, and her face was swathed in a knowing smile. She had read my mind, and I responded with a weak smile of my own and a squeeze of her hand. As I did so, Selene turned her head and I saw her smile disappear instantly as her eyes fell upon me. As I watched, she sat bolt upright in her wheelchair, startled.

Her reaction was hardly what I wanted – not the beaming smile of recognition I had dreamt of so many times. Indeed, I was not even certain that she had recognised me as I had worn swimming shorts on the only other occasion we had met.

Her mood changed suddenly as I realised that she did know who I was, but still no smile of welcome crossed her face. It was more of puzzlement, tinged with apprehension – perhaps even a little fear. Was I there to tell the world of her stabbing her Italian Barone? Whatever had caused it, the mood passed almost as quickly as it had appeared, and her lovely smile slowly lit up her face.

If Marshall had been watching, rather than holding court, he might have noted a rather odd sight – Selene smiling at me, me smiling at Selene, and Julie smiling at both of us, yet not one of us making any move to meet up. This tableau remained static for several moments before Selene started to mouth some words at me.

"Did you get that," asked Julie "One of my best friends at school was deaf, and we both learned to lip-read very early."

"No. I thought she was mouthing my name, but it didn't seem to fit."

"*Later*," she explained. "She says she'll catch up with you later."

"Ah, thanks," I said, as I continued to smile and stare at Serene. "OK. Let's go back and join your friends."

As we walked, Julie said, "You're right. She's very pretty."

"She is," I had to agree. "And so too are you. You look lovely tonight. I wanted to tell you earlier, but didn't get the chance."

She turned a slightly flushed face towards me. "Well thank you, Martin."

Our eyes met, and we just stood looking at each other for a few seconds. I was a heartbeat away from sweeping her in my arms and kissing her. And I felt it was almost certain she would respond. It was such a close thing. For a split second, my life could have taken a very different turn, but my journey was nearly over, and my course set fair.

A quarter of an hour later, dinner was announced and we all trooped to the table we had been allocated, where we were joined by other friends who sailed the same class of yachts. The Sailors' Widows Club was now well represented on the table. It was a disparate group in age, class, and even looks, but its members all had one thing in common – each had a partner with divided loyalties, for which she had to compete. Golf widows and anglers' wives experience similar problems, but a racing yacht is a large tangible object, with a physical life of its own – easy to love, easy to hate. It is a fickle and exacting mistress, demanding large quantities of affection, time and money.

The gulf between the sailors and their land-based partners became even more evident when the Squadron's Commodore started his speech. He peppered it with anecdotes and in-jokes about the races, which had the crews helpless with laughter, whilst their partners looked on with bemused faces.

Port was passed around, and the tables began to break up with some members leaving to smoke out on the lawns. I felt Julie touch my shoulder and then she whispered in my ear, "Go get her boy." I turned towards her, smiled, and squeezed her hand once again. I got up slowly and walked away from the table with as much confidence as I could raise.

I had gone only a few yards when Selene herself nearly collided with me. "Hi Martin," she said, with a beaming smile on her face. As you might imagine, my heart was now in overdrive and for the moment, I was tongue-tied. But she had remembered my name. A good start, I thought.

"We've got to talk," she continued eagerly. "Let's try to find somewhere quieter. Follow me." She punched her hand down onto the drive wheel of her chair and, turning through 180 degrees, started towards some unoccupied tables on the far side of the bar.

"Should I push you?" I bent down to ask in her ear.

"If you like," she said. "I can manage, but if it would make you feel more ... connected."

An odd choice of words, I thought. Was she flirting already? Did she ever stop? She seemed to be picking up exactly from where we left off all those weeks ago.

She stopped by an empty table and I pulled out a chair to sit beside her.

"It's good to see you again," I started rather formally.

"What are you doing here, Martin?" she asked, serious for a moment. "I know that it's no coincidence. I've heard you've been trying to trace me."

For some reason, I hadn't expected that. "Who told you?" I asked.

"Justin Courtney. I spoke with him a week or so ago. He told me you'd visited him at his house."

"That's true. I'll tell you all about it sometime."

"But why, Martin? Why have you been chasing me around?"

"I was concerned for your wellbeing."

"*Concerned for my wellbeing?*" She almost shouted this out – a question.

"I thought you'd been injured – maybe badly. At one time, I was convinced you'd been murdered and dumped in the lake. I simply had to find out."

"Why should you think that?"

"When I called at the house, a couple of days after we met, the place had been trashed. There was blood, lots of it, out on the terrace – everywhere. Something terrible seemed to have happened."

"And do you know what had happened?" she asked apprehensively.

"I know now."

"How?"

"Guiseppi has told me all about it," I said.

The blood was draining from her face. "You've spoken to him?"

"I went to see him ..."

"You went to see Pino?" She interrupted, amazed and not a little concerned. "In Italy? You went to see him in Italy?"

I nodded. "Don't forget I have a place out there – only two or three hours' drive away."

"What did he say? What did he tell you had happened?"

"He told me everything, Selene." She was now white as a sheet.

"Don't worry," I assured her quickly. "He told me in confidence. He doesn't intend taking any action against you. It's in the past – forgotten."

We were both silent for a while as she recovered her composure.

"And is that all, Martin? Is that the only reason you've been following me?"

I knew I would have to answer such a question at some time. I just hadn't expected it so soon, and I squirmed as I blushed and started to stammer, "I ... Well, I wanted to see you again. I liked you. And ... well, I suppose that's why I wanted to be certain you were OK."

"You fancied me, Martin, didn't you?" she asked, now with a twinkle in her eyes.

I had no place to hide. "Yes," I admitted with a shy smile. "I hope you're not cross."

"I'm not cross, Martin," she laughed. "I'm flattered, and I want to hear all about your efforts to find me. The very least I can do is to give you some time. But I must go back to Jim now."

"Jim?" I queried.

"Sir James Marshall," she said, putting on a mocking haughty voice. "He'll be wondering what's happened to me."

"You came with him then?"

She looked at me for a moment or two with that teasing smile that I remembered so well. "Yes," she said eventually – assertively, almost challenging me to raise some objection.

I said nothing, and she continued, "He'll be outside, I expect, with a large glass of port in his hand and a giant cigar stuck in his mouth. Why don't you come and meet him?"

"I don't think I want to," I said. "How long are you staying on the island?"

"Two or three days I think. Oh, wait a minute." She paused for several seconds, thinking. "Do you remember, the day we met, we were going to take a boat ride around the lake. But I couldn't go and offered you a rain check. Would you like to cash it in now?"

I was confused and asked, "How's that?"

"Jim has a motor yacht – as well as his sailing yacht. We're going out in it tomorrow. He wants to take it down the coast for some lunch. Don't ask me where – I've forgotten. He's only just thought about it and I don't think he's arranged a crew, so he'd be quite happy to have you along."

"Hang on. I can't crew for him. I may be able to row a small boat around a lake, but I know nothing about sailing at sea."

"Oh well, I'll talk to him." She smiled, and then said, "I'm sure he'll let you come along anyway."

"One of the guys I'm with tonight is a sailor. I'm sure he could crew for him – so long as he doesn't have a race. Do you think he could manage another couple?"

"No problem. I'm sure he will. It's a big boat. Let's go and see him."

She noticed my hesitation and cut short any discussion by turning her chair and wheeling off towards the exit to the lawns. "Come on," she shouted after her.

I followed, with my anxiety rising as we approached the big man. He was just as Selene had described. The bright red glow of the largest cigar in the world acted as a beacon for us and as we arrived, we were greeted by a dense cloud of smoke that gave out an overpowering sweet aroma.

"Ah, here she is. We were wondering where you'd got to, my love," Sir James bellowed as Selene pulled in beside him.

"I ran into an old friend," she explained. "This is Martin ... I'm sorry, Martin, I can't remember your surname."

"Ramsay," I reminded her.

"Martin Ramsay ... yes." Turning to me, she continued, "Let me introduce Sir James Marshall", and then after a short pause ... "my stepfather."

If this revelation was intended to put me at my ease, then it failed miserably. I immediately recalled how, very early in our first meeting, Selene had been very critical of her stepfather. She had been upset as she remembered how badly he had treated both her and her mother. And hadn't Justin said something about abuse?

"You thought I was her beau – didn't you, young man," he roared and beamed at the laughter from his cluster of acolytes.

"I had no idea, Sir. I hadn't thought about it," was the best I could manage.

Selene sprang to my rescue. "It's a long story, but I once promised Martin a boat trip. Would you mind if he joined us tomorrow?"

"Sure," he agreed. "We'll need a crew."

"I'm sorry, Sir. That's not me. I'm not a sailor – I'd just be there for the ride, I'm afraid."

"Pity," he said. "And call me Jim. Everyone else here does."

"If you need a sailor, I've come here tonight with a good one," I offered. "Perhaps he and his girlfriend could join us?"

He looked around at his entourage. "You lot are all going back tomorrow, aren't you?" he bawled. They all nodded.

"No stamina," he said in a loud stage whisper in our direction. "OK. The more the merrier. Someone recommended a restaurant in Chichester Harbour and I've booked a table. I'll give them a tinkle when I know exactly how many we are."

"Sounds great, Jim," I said. "Can I bring anything?"

"Just that crew man. I'll need him. What's his name?"

"Brad. He's Australian."

"Ah well. I suppose we can't be too fussy. OK, Martin. Tomorrow morning – bright and early. 8.00 am. The boat's called Sea Mist and she's berthed in the Shepards Wharf Marina. Don't be late."

"Thanks. I'll be there. Enjoy the rest of the evening." I put my hand on Selene's shoulder and said gently, "Bye. See you tomorrow. And thanks."

I recounted all that had transpired to Julie and Brad, who both happily agreed to join the following day's trip. I felt good. Things had gone well. I could not understand why Selene was with a man she seemed to loathe, but at least it was no romantic liaison. And I would be with her again tomorrow. I was a happy man and got in the next round of drinks.

It turned out to be the first of many more rounds, as a carousel of Brad's sailing mates came and went. I watched Sir James and Selene leave a good hour before the Commodore finally closed the event. Brad knew the Sea Mist – "It's a really big boat," he said. And he had frequently used the marina and gave me instructions to find it as we were all leaving.

"See you both tomorrow morning then. Don't be late," I insisted.

"And thanks again for arranging tonight," I added.

Chapter 18

My mobile's alarm was sounding at its most insistent level before it managed to wake me and I reached out to silence it, not wishing to disturb the whole house at six o'clock. I was up almost immediately as I wanted to grab some breakfast, and still had to find the marina and the boat. I dressed as swiftly as possible in the bundle of clothes I had put out the previous night. With all the alcohol inside me, I remember laughing out aloud as I put together the pathetic collection that would have to pass for my sailing kit – a clean white shirt, navy blue shorts, grey socks and a pair of white tennis shoes. In the cold light of day, it was not so funny, and I wondered what withering remark Sir James would come up with when he saw me. Then I suddenly realised it might be cool outside at this time of the morning, and also on board, so I grabbed a sweater before quietly slipping out of the front door.

    The roads were deserted, and I began to doubt whether I would find anywhere open for breakfast, but life was already stirring as I reached town. I found a cafe open at the far end of the High Street and ordered a full English breakfast as I felt I needed to put some bulk on top of last night's liquids. I was just finishing off some toast and marmalade when, through the front window, I caught sight of a young man pushing Selene in her wheelchair, with Sir James striding alongside. I looked at my watch. It was twenty-to-eight. I had to get going and called for the bill.

Shepards Wharf was only a few minutes' walk further along the front. An elderly man, his grizzled face witness to many years of open sea sailing, was seated in a small office inside the entrance. I poked my head round the open door. "Sea Mist?" I queried.

He pointed along the corridor. "Outer pontoon," was all he said.

I need not have bothered. As soon as I was out into the Marina, I had only to make my way to the largest motor launch visible. As I hopped on board, Selene greeted me with, "Hi Martin." She had been decanted from her wheelchair and was seated in the well of the open rear deck, where I joined her.

"Are your friends coming?" she asked. "I think we're nearly ready ... Oh, that might be one of them now."

I followed her eyes and caught sight of Brad running along the pontoon towards the boat.

"I'm sorry," he said breathlessly, as he clambered on board. "Bit of a blue."

I looked at my watch. "Don't worry," I said. "You're not late. But what's a `blue' in the English language?"

Brad snorted a laugh. "An argument. I've just had a row with Julie. She's not coming – thinks it's going to be too rough for her. I've gotta say, she does get seasick easily."

At that moment, Sir James's head appeared over the coping of the deck above. "Is everybody on board? Do I have my crew?" he boomed.

"Yes. Everyone's on board," Selene shouted up to him.

Another head appeared – the young man I had seen earlier, pushing Selene.

"This is Ben everyone," Sir James roared. "He's our engineer. OK."

I piped up then, with a rather cheeky opening, "Good morning, Jim." I turned and pointed to Julie's boyfriend – maybe now her ex-boyfriend. "And this is Brad. There's not much he doesn't know about boats and sailing. He's your crew, Sir."

"Welcome aboard, Brad. Join us up here, if you will. I'd like to get this show on the road."

A quarter of an hour later, I was sitting beside Selene, her blond locks flowing out almost horizontally behind her as the boat sped out into the Solent. Our bodies were bulky, the skip having ordered us to don some unattractive yellow waterproof gear and cumbersome lifejackets – just about the least sexy gear imaginable. The boat's powerful engines were located somewhere below us. Their noise, along with the loud *clunk* as the boat slapped into each wave, precluded any meaningful conversation, although we did occasionally manage a few shouted words.

After a while, I felt Selene's hand seeking mine and willingly – oh, so willingly – I took hold of it. I turned towards her and smiled. Suddenly, I felt more relaxed than I had done in weeks. My quest, all the thought, work and travel, had ended in success. Selene was alive and well, and her hand was in mine. I felt on top of the world, and I laughed aloud. She saw me and shouted in my ear, "What are you laughing at?"

"I'm happy. That's all." She smiled, and I continued to laugh. I couldn't stop.

The night before, I had caught the same weather forecast that Julie had presumably heard and, after we had been going for an hour or so, the wind began to get up. Large gouts of spray were coming aboard and the wind was cold on our hands and faces. I began to wonder whether we should go below but with the violent motion of the boat, getting Selene there might be a problem. I let go of her hand and put my arm around her.

"Should we go below," I suggested in her ear.

"No, I'm fine. It's exhilarating, isn't it?"

"You're warm enough?" I asked.

"I am for the moment, yes. But I wouldn't mind a drink – some coffee perhaps. I'm afraid you're the spare hand today, and it's your job. The galley is one deck down and for'ard. You'll have to get orders from the others up on the bridge."

"Right," I agreed.

As I got up, I placed my heart in my mouth for a moment and bent over to give her a fleeting kiss, which she accepted on her lips. Feeling ridiculously happy, I skipped off to the gangway and the staircase leading to the upper deck.

Naturally, Sir James was at the wheel. Except that, there was no large wheel as we are used to seeing on traditional sailing ships, but a console filled with a bewildering collection of knobs, dials and joysticks. Brad was studying some charts on a nearby table and turned as I entered. "Hi, Mart. Selene sent you packing already?"

I chose to ignore both the remark and the truncation of my name. "She tells me I've been designated "water wallah" for the day, so can I get anyone a coffee ... or tea perhaps?"

Sir James looked at his watch. "What the hell, we're only a couple of hours off lunch now. You can get me a gin and tonic – long and strong, with ice and lemon. You'll find them all in the fridge."

"Right, Jim ... Brad?"

"I'll have the same, mate."

"I must say, this is a great boat you've got here, Jim.

"Yeah. I'm very fond of it. I've used it more than once. It's not mine though – I rent it by the day. Or should I say, one of my Companies rents it for me and my clients – that's you lot."

So that was it – some sort of tax wheeze. I was suddenly aware that I was in a different world, one I had never moved in and hardly recognised. I was now hopeful of some sort of relationship with Selene, but could I keep up with her wealthy and high-flying friends and the circles she moved in? Somehow, it didn't trouble me right then, and I would happily play the part of waiter for the day.

"What about Ben? Where is he?"

"He'll probably want the same if I know him," said Sir James. "But you'd better check. He'll be playing with his babies down below – just follow the noise. And the galley is under here, two decks down."

He sounded strangely subdued, but he suddenly raised his voice, "Fuck this bloody thing. I can't move in it." As he spoke, he roughly untied the straps of his lifejacket and shrugged it off. "It makes me so bloody hot," he added, as he flung it into a corner.

It was Brad who spoke up, "It's important, Jim. We should wear them at all times."

"Captain's prerogative," he barked.

"I'm going to insist," Brad continued.

"Insist away," Sir James said gruffly, defying any further argument.

I wasn't going to get involved, and turned to leave, "I'll get the drinks ..."

I had assumed that Ben's babies were the engines and had no difficulty in finding him, where he confirmed his order. In the galley, non-alcoholic provisions were sparse and I could find no coffee, but I made a hot chocolate for Selene. By the time I had delivered them all, I could see that we were approaching the shore.

We chugged slowly along the fingers of the harbour to Bosham and were fortunate to find room to tie up at the small pontoon at the quayside. Brad and I manhandled Selene ashore and settled her into her wheelchair, while Sir James strode on ahead up the village towards his chosen restaurant.

It was crowded, but money and a knighthood had worked their magic and we were shepherded to a round table in a bay window overlooking a pleasant courtyard. I secured a chair next to Selene and Sir James settled himself opposite. With the promise of excellent food, everything seemed set for a happy and entertaining couple of hours.

But Sir James and Selene had argued before we all met up, as I already knew had Brad and Julie. Hangovers from these may well have influenced events, for Sir James was a very different companion to the ebullient man I had met on the previous evening. He sat impassive, silent throughout most of the meal, with his thoughts somewhere else, seemingly impervious to all efforts to lighten the mood. It made for a sadly sombre affair, which the remaining four of us could not lift, despite the excellent food and wine.

At one point, I wondered if he was sick. This was partly due to the pallor of his face, which had lost much of its high colour. But I suddenly realised that it was also because I was beginning to feel rather unwell myself. It was too soon to be anything in the food, I thought. Maybe I was an even worse sailor than I had imagined.

Eventually, Sir James awoke from his reverie and asked for the bill. Assuming that we would all be responsible for our share, I dug out my wallet and held it loosely on the table. Sir James flicked a finger at it, saying curtly, "Put it away, Martin. I told you, you're all my esteemed clients today. The company's paying."

I hesitated, looking around at the others. They stared back at me non-committedly, and Sir James once again flicked his finger at my wallet. It seemed I was outvoted, and I shrugged and put it away. Having worked for many years in the building industry, I know how jollies and freebies work and it was good to be at the receiving end for a change, but in no way did it alter my opinion of the man.

Back on the quayside, it was immediately evident that the wind had increased still more since, even in the shelter of the harbour, the boat was heaving at the pontoon and we manhandled Selene aboard with considerable difficulty. She was full of spirit, and I groaned inwardly as she insisted on the same exposed seat at the rear. My stomach was churning and a nauseous feeling was beginning to deaden my mind. I knew from experience that I was close to vomiting, but all I wanted to do was to lie down and sleep.

To give him his due, Sir James came to my rescue. He had noted my colour and guessed my plight, and he took decisive command. He would sit with Selene, leaving the navigation in the safe hands of Ben and Brad. He ordered Ben, who knew the boat better than anyone, to find me a bed, "somewhere close to a toilet – try one of the rear cabins." Ben was an odd-looking fellow and had not said much during lunch, but he made sure that I was comfortable, showed me the bathroom and placed a mug of water close by me. It was not long before I was emptying much of the contents of my stomach, which relieved many of the symptoms, but left me overwhelmingly sleepy.

I am not sure how long I slept – probably only half an hour or so. Neither am I sure what had woken me. Certainly, I was close to vomiting again, and my first port of call was another hurried trip to the bathroom. But it could equally have been the motion of the boat as it now shuddered violently each time it crashed into a wave. Or it might have been the noise from the engines, or the swish of the water as it passed. But it could also have been from a new noise that I had not noticed before – voices from the deck above. They were raised. The two of them were quarrelling again.

I could not resist listening but, with all the other noises, could only make out the occasional word. It continued for several minutes, the voice levels rising and falling as the argument progressed. Finally, the sound reached new heights, with both of them screeching abuse at each other. And with this came something new – a scratchy noise, something scraping along the deck. And then, very suddenly, the shouting died. At the same time, I thought I heard a muffled splash but with all the other noises, I couldn't be sure. Later events may have influenced this recollection, but I held my breath, attempting to hear any little thing. I leant over the bunk and pressed my ear to the bulkhead, but could hear nothing from the deck above.

After about five minutes, I could bear it no longer and summoned the strength to get up. But, just as I was putting on my trainers, I heard a screech. With only one shoe on, I rushed for the door and staircase. As I came out on deck, I collided with Ben who was coming down from the deck above. Selene was beside herself, screaming uncontrollably.

"What's up," I shouted, and then, unable to see Sir James and fearing the worst, "Where's Jim?"

Selene said nothing but shook her head, as she continued to scream.

"Stop the boat," I shouted to Ben, who turned and scrambled off, on the run.

Only a few seconds later, the motors died. Then they started again as the boat was turned through 180 degrees. Ben must have taken the helm then, as Brad joined us at the rear.

"Keep a lookout for man overboard," he said. "I'll be on the bridge with Ben. Martin, could you go onto the foredeck? It's a bit exposed, I'm afraid, but you'll get a better view up there."

As he was leaving, his head suddenly shot round and he shouted, "Don't tell me he'd taken off his lifebelt again?"

"I'm afraid so," I said. I had already spotted it in the corner of the deck.

"We haven't got much time then," said Brad glumly, as he wheeled off.

"Selene," I said as I put my arms around her. "We have to start searching." Her screams had subsided, but she was holding a tissue to her nose, snivelling. "I know," she managed.

"Before we do, what happened exactly?"

"He jumped – just got up and jumped overboard. I couldn't stop him ..."

"When?" I interrupted, "When did he jump? Did you scream as soon as you saw him jump?"

"Yes. Oh, Martin, I couldn't do anything about it. I felt so helpless."

"You're sure he didn't jump earlier? You screamed as soon as he jumped? It makes a difference to the size of the search area."

"Yes, of course," she said uncertainly, frowning. "I screamed when he jumped."

"Right," I said. I was not entirely convinced, but this was no time to argue. "You see what you can from here. I'm going up front."

It was raw on the forecastle deck. Spray was driving over the bow with each wave. My oilskin jacket offered some protection, but I was soaked through and shivering within five minutes. The spray also stung my eyes, which hampered my vision, and I decided I would be more use higher up.

The bridge was a hive of activity. Ben had the helm, whilst Brad was calculating a mass of coordinates and drawing grid lines for a search pattern. At the same time, he was talking on the radio to several other boats, coast guards and onshore rescue centres. I decided not to disturb them, and left immediately to climb up to the sun deck, which was still exposed to the wind, but spared all but the lightest spray. It gave me a far better viewing point, and I could see that Ben was steering a reverse course, following along our wake, which was still faintly visible. I spotted a chunky set of binoculars in a holder lashed to the forward bulkhead. They proved to be rather too powerful to use for the search but would be invaluable for investigating any sighting.

For several minutes, my eyes swept an area of sea about twenty metres in front of the bow, but it wasn't easy. As each wave rolled by, I had only a short time to scour the trough before it was obscured by the next wave that arrived. I had failed to spot anything by the time Ben again turned the boat through 180 degrees, presumably into the next line of Brad's search pattern. With my eyes glued to the sea, I did some mental arithmetic. Following Selene's scream, we can't have continued sailing for more than five minutes before Brad had stopped the boat and turned it around. In this sea, I doubted if we could be doing more than about five or six knots, so a quick calculation meant that we wouldn't have travelled more than about half a mile, less than a thousand metres.

A helicopter was the first help to arrive – swooping down over us so low that I ducked instinctively. A few moments later, we were joined by a couple of yachts that had been in the area and had picked up our mayday call. A lifeboat was the next to arrive and very soon, the whole area was bristling with helicopters and boats of all types and sizes. I was cold now and decided to leave them to it.

I descended to the bridge, where Ben and Brad were busy handing over control of the search to the experts, shouting out a stream of incomprehensible figures. I had nothing to offer and joined Selene on the deck below. She had recovered most of her composure now, but she was shivering from the cold. Somehow, I had to get her into the forward lounge – but how? She was safe whilst she was strapped into the static seat, but if I unbuckled her, she would be at the mercy of the violent motions of the deck. I fetched her wheelchair but, with only two hands, I could not keep it still enough to prepare it and then lift her into it. I thought I might be able simply to carry her inside, but as soon as I tried, I started to stagger dangerously. Oddly, she began to laugh and then shouted at me to leave her where she was.

"It's too dangerous," she squealed. "I'll be OK. Come here. Give me a cuddle."

I needed no second invitation, although I wondered whether I had any body heat to be of use to her. Our oilskins and lifejackets prevented any great passion, but I was happy enough in the embrace, and eventually, we did manage to generate enough heat between us for her shivering to subside.

"Has anyone spotted anything?" She asked, serious once more.

"Not yet. I fear he's gone. Was he a strong swimmer, do you know?"

She shrugged. "He could swim. I remember when I was a kid. But he's a lot heavier now, and in seas like this ... I don't know."

"Well, we'll know soon enough. Are you OK? I don't know how long we'll have to stay out here."

As I said this, Brad's head appeared over the bridge bulkhead. "We're going back to Cowes," he announced. "We can't add much to the search party, and we're running low on fuel. Are you OK, Selene?"

"She's alright," I answered for her. "But she's cold, and I can't move her inside by myself."

"I'm fine," Selene shouted. "Don't worry about me."

I simply shrugged.

"Call me if you need me," said Brad as he went back into the bridge.

Less than an hour later, we were tying up at the same berth we had left in the morning. A reception party was already waiting on the pontoon. Somehow, the press had got to hear of the incident, and a couple of eager cub reporters were waving mobiles and notebooks to attract attention.

But a posse of officials were also there, and we were told to prepare to be de-briefed.

Chapter 19

Each of us was led to separate rooms for individual interviews. Whilst Ben and Brad were seen in the Marina, a young security guard led me, pushing Selene, to a nearby office building. Leaving Selene seated in her chair, he showed me into a large room where I sat alone at a conference table for about five minutes before a tall, elegant man entered. He was elderly, with a gaunt, pale face and was dressed immaculately in a dark grey suit. His sombre appearance was lifted somewhat by a shock of thick iron-grey hair and a bright blue bow tie, and he smiled pleasantly as he introduced himself as John Harkness. He placed a voice recorder between us and spent a few silent seconds fiddling with it until he was sure it was functioning properly.

"I'm sorry," he started. "This may seem premature – I hope to heaven that your friend is found safe and well, but I understand that he's been in the water for several hours now." He paused and sighed heavily. "Realistically, although we should continue to live in hope, we must prepare for the worst, and that's where I come in. The right time is always difficult, of course, but we find it important to gather evidence as soon as possible after such an event – whilst memories are fresh."

I nodded acceptance, and he continued, "We're just coppers. Taking statements is what we do. Others may be involved later – the Coroner's Office, and maybe even the Marine Accident Investigation Branch. I don't know, but a statement made now will be invaluable to any of them. Right?"

I nodded again.

"OK," he said and then announced the date, time, place and our names for the benefit of the recorder.

"Let's start with a few details about yourself." With these recorded, he asked me to describe my day, "from start to finish, please".

He listened intently as I spoke, occasionally jotting some remark into his notebook. I found no difficulty in recalling the day's events in reasonable detail – until I came to my enforced period in a bunk below decks. I explained how I had spent the time moving seamlessly in and out of sleep, and that any recollections were very hazy. I told him I remembered hearing voices from the deck above, but not that they had been raised in anger, nor did I mention the possibility that I might have heard the splash or the delay I had noted between that and Selene's scream. It was all very unclear in my mind, and I decided to stick to Selene's story. I had no wish to conflict with her evidence.

"Fine. Thank you very much. That gives me a clear picture."

He paused then, flipping through the notes he had taken. Every so often, he would ask for some clarification or a personal opinion. "You say Sir James was quiet over lunch – I believe you described him as 'subdued'. Can you account for this?"

"I'm not sure," I replied. "I think he and Selene had quarrelled earlier, but I don't know what it was about. He seemed very preoccupied."

"And after lunch – oh, did he pay the bill for everyone?"

"Yes. He said it was his party."

"After lunch, did he offer to look after Selene for the return journey?"

"Again – yes. He could see I wasn't well, and ordered me below."

"Now ... you said you could hear them talking on the deck above. Could you hear what they were saying? Do you know what they were talking about?"

"No. I was much too close to the engines. There was too much noise."

"But you heard her scream?"

"Oh yes. I'll remember that for some time. They heard it up in the wheelhouse too."

He flipped his book. "And ... you say when you got onto the deck, his life jacket was still in the rack. Are you certain he wasn't wearing one? Surely it's mandatory?"

"There was one in the corner of the deck, and I'm pretty sure it was his. I saw him take it off in the morning, and I doubt if he put it on after the break for lunch. There was quite a row about him taking it off. The crew told him it was mandatory and tried to get him to put it back on. But he's a tough man, and he doesn't react well to anyone ordering him about. What could they do?"

Harkness thought for a while, placing a tick in his notebook. "OK," he said finally. "I think that'll do for now. When will you be leaving the island?"

I shrugged. "I don't know. Tomorrow maybe. It depends on what happens here. I haven't made any particular plans yet."

"Well, I have your address if I need to get in touch." He flipped through his notebook once again. "Somewhere in Norfolk, wasn't it?"

"Yes. It's my father's address. I'm going through a divorce, and I'm staying with him for now. I don't know how long I'll be there, but he'll always be able to get in touch with me."

"Right," he said. After a short pause, he leant forward, "Interview terminated 18.08," he announced and switched off the recorder. The silence that followed was broken by a sudden loud knock at the door. As his head swung round, and with no words of permission, it was flung open and a young, rosy-cheeked uniformed policewoman almost ran into the room to announce, "They've found him."

"Thank you, Debra," Harkness said quietly, but with a smile on his face. "That is good news. How is he?"

"I'm sorry, Sir. I don't know anything more."

"Very well. I'll see you at the Station shortly."

She read this as a dismissal and left the room. "I'm surprised," Harkness said. "Pleasantly surprised. I didn't expect him to survive in those conditions, especially with no lifejacket."

"No," I agreed. I could think of nothing more to say. My sickness had passed almost as quickly as it had begun, but I felt numb – drained by the ever-changing events of the day.

Harkness got up and offered me his hand. "If we were at the Station, I'd offer you a cup of tea, but there are no facilities here. We've just borrowed this place. I must get on now, so let's go and find the rest of your party."

Selene was still being interviewed, and Harkness went in only to learn that she would be another twenty minutes or so. His reference to a cup of tea had made me conscious of a very empty stomach, and I had to get something into it. I asked Harkness to get a message to Selene that I was going out for a bite to eat and would be back for her in half an hour.

The weather had eased, and I found myself unconsciously walking towards the teashop that I knew so well. I admit to being a creature of habit but I wonder, as I write now, whether it was a subconscious attempt to meet up again with Julie. She would make an ideal sounding board, I thought. I was confused as to Selene's involvement in the accident and felt a need to talk it over with someone.

She was not in the cafe, of course. I sat alone at our favourite table and ordered a coffee and a plate of scrambled eggs. It all went down far too quickly and, as I was scouring the plate, I realised that it was coming up to time for dinner. I felt I had only taken the edge off my appetite and resolved to take Selene to a good restaurant. We had eaten well at lunchtime but, with all the subsequent events, I guessed she too would be hungry.

Her interview had only just concluded when I arrived to pick her up.

"Hi," I said. "All finished?"

"Yup. Let's go."

"You've heard they've found Jim? We don't know where he is – or how he is. Do you want to go and see him?"

She pulled a face. "No. I couldn't face it today. Let's leave it 'till the morning."

As I gently bumped her down the shallow entrance steps, I suggested, "Shall we go and have something to eat then?"

She turned to me and smiled. "I was told you'd already gone out to eat," she accused.

"I did have a small plate of something," I agreed sheepishly. "But I was so hungry. My stomach was empty from the sickness. We'll both need some dinner – no?"

"Yes," she agreed. "I believe I could manage some. But not yet. I'm not doing anything before I've cleaned up. I need a shower and a change of clothes."

"You certainly do," I said, holding my nose. She slapped my hand.

"Which way to your hotel?" I asked.

"It's not far. This way," she said, pointing along the High Street in the direction of The Parade. After about five minutes, she indicated a block of apartments with large glass balconies protruding out towards the sea. "Here we are," she announced.

My face must have been a picture as I pushed her into the top-floor penthouse. "Nice eh?" she smiled. "I hope your place is half as good." It was a large apartment and put my pathetic room to shame. It had floor-to-ceiling windows along the entire frontage, offering fantastic uninterrupted views of the Solent, with yachts bobbing at their buoys in the foreground. It had been designed in the modern open plan fashion, with stylish minimalist furniture – not homely, but interesting, attractive and practical. Selene wheeled herself into one of the bedrooms, whilst I started to explore the main living area. Eventually, I found what I was looking for – a drinks cabinet. With ice and lemon from the fridge in the kitchen, I was able to make myself a long and much-needed gin and tonic.

I had just settled myself down into a deep comfortable chair, when I heard a call from the bedroom, "Martin."

I struggled out of the chair with the drink in my hand and walked to the bedroom door.

"Yes?" I shouted.

"Come here, Martin."

"Are you decent?"

"Oh, come in you silly boy."

My heart was over-revving as I opened the door and peered in, wondering what to expect. In the event, I didn't know whether to be disappointed or relieved. She was still seated in her wheelchair but now enveloped in a fluffy white bathrobe. As I entered, she said, "You'll have to give me a hand, Martin."

"Of course," I said and then stopped still, looking helpless – not knowing what to do, waiting for instructions.

"I'll show you how we do this," she started. "There's a special plastic stool in the shower, which I have to take wherever I go. But this wheelchair's too big for the opening, and I need a double lift to get there."

She paused for a moment and then continued, "Would you mind getting a chair from the kitchen."

I put down my drink and fetched an upright wooden chair, which she asked to be placed by the shower, and then to lift her into it. She is not a tall girl, and I had always known that her body was slight, but I was surprised by how easily I was able to lift her. My mind reverted to our meeting all those weeks ago, and I was reminded of that first moment of shock when Guiseppi had lifted her from her sun lounger.

The narrow shower door made the next move rather more awkward. As I stretched over to place her down on her stool, her robe rucked up and exposed the foothills of her right breast. It was only a fleeting glimpse, for the gown closed again as I set her down, but I could feel my desire stirring and gave her lips a brief kiss on my way to straightening up.

Perhaps this kiss gave her notice of my arousal, for she slapped my wrist and said with one of her cheeky smiles, "Get out of here, you naughty boy."

As I backed out of the shower, she added, "Thank you, Martin, you'll get used to it."

I almost skipped out of the bedroom to meet up with my gin and tonic. My journey was at an end – all my goals achieved. I had found my goddess, alive and well, and she had now accepted her worshipper as a friend and suitor. I was walking on air.

It was close to another hour before I pushed Selene through the crowded throng of al fresco diners in front of the restaurant she recommended. She was evidently a well-regarded customer, and there was no shortage of waiters soon buzzing around and finding us a discrete table. I have a penchant for soup and couldn't resist the french onion, whilst Selene chose some pâté.

We were only halfway through these when I recognised the unmistakable Aussie accent of Brad as he entered with four of his sailing buddies. They didn't notice us as they passed and were shown to a table at the far end of the restaurant.

Our main course had yet to arrive when Brad did finally catch sight of us. He excused himself to his guests, and strode over to our table, looking grim.

"I'm real gutted about your stepfather, Selene," he said. "I'm so sorry."

Selene and I looked at each other. Then I said, "Perhaps you haven't heard, Brad. They've found him."

He looked at each of us in turn, his suntanned face turning to the colour of ancient parchment. After a few seconds, he started again, "It may be that you haven't heard the very latest news. He's dead, I'm afraid."

I watched Selene's reaction. But her face was a blank canvas – impassive. I couldn't read it, but I continued to try as Brad resumed. "He was alive when they fished him out – but only just. The paramedics worked on him in the lifeboat, but he suffered a massive heart attack well before they were close to the shore. It must have been the effort of keeping afloat – and the cold, I figure. Anyway, they couldn't save him."

Then, after a short pause, "I'm sorry to break it to you like this, Selene. I had no idea that you hadn't heard."

"Thanks, Brad. I'd lost him once already today. A second time makes little difference."

"Where's Julie, Brad," I asked. "I didn't see her when you came in."

"No," he said gloomily. "She'd gone by the time we got back – left me a note."

I didn't press him further. I could guess from his face what it had said.

He left us then with, "I'll see you guys. I guess there'll be more questions in the morning."

The death of someone close can have unpredictable effects. Fits of uncontrolled laughter are one of the least expected. I have seen it before, and it happened again that evening. Selene had already served several hours of grief – if indeed she ever had any to spend on her stepfather! Even before we had finished eating our main course, we had already polished off a bottle of white wine, and I now ordered a red to enjoy with some cheese. And enjoy it we did. Despite Brad's news, our conversation began to flow more freely, lighter, flirtatious, and full of fun. Stiff black coffees failed to sober us up and, to the amusement of the staff, we left the almost empty restaurant amid gales of laughter.

Fortunately, we had only about a hundred yards to walk, although my inebriated state and inexperience with the wheelchair meant that a wayward course probably doubled that figure. She may have been feigning it somewhat, but Selene seemed incapable of inserting the key in the lock, and I had to take over the task. This raised the laughter to new heights, causing me to stumble and lose control of the wheelchair, which tipped up and deposited Selene in a jumbled heap on the floor. Fortunately, it started her off laughing even louder, so I knew she was unhurt. I kicked the door shut behind me and joined her on the floor.

    I think we had both known from the very start of the evening that this was destined to be the night we would become lovers for the first time. Many people might well consider that the evening's excessive quantities of food and wine would make for less than ideal foreplay, but I am not convinced – alcohol emboldens the nervous and the shy. Between us, we managed to sort out the jumble that was her useless, but lovely, limbs and we fell together spontaneously and joyously. During the coming months, with tutorage from an expert and experiments of our own, I was to learn of myriad ways of making love to and pleasuring a paraplegic. But that first night was nothing more than a hilarious mixture of trial, fumbling error and convulsive laughter which fell away only as, all too soon, a sort of climax was reached. Somehow, it made some perverse sense of such a ridiculous, but wondrous, activity as the act of sex.

    Our high spirits continued as we somehow muddled through the process of readying our partly dressed bodies for bed. The mirth had hardly subsided by the time, totally exhausted from the day's events, from the free-flowing wine, and from our more recent exertions, we fell asleep in each other's arms.

Chapter 20

We were awoken by the insistent ringing of Selene's mobile, which for obvious reasons she always keeps close to hand. This rude awakening pre-empted a more sober attempt at the previous night's activity.

The call was from the police station, asking her to call in as soon as possible. They would give no details, but said it was urgent. We wolfed down bowls of cereal, and I wheeled her to their small office at the end of the High Street. A young, rather effeminate-looking police officer was the only occupant. He got up from behind the counter and headed straight for Selene.

"Good morning, Mrs Courtney," he greeted. "Thanks for coming so quickly, but there's been a development since I last saw you." I guessed that he was the officer who had interviewed her the previous afternoon, and he looked very solemn now, "I'm sorry to have to tell you that your stepfather died yesterday."

Before he could continue, Selene cut in quickly, "I know. We heard last night."

"Oh, I see." He seemed relieved, but continued, "Were you told what happened – the cause of his death?"

"Yes. Well, very briefly. They said it was a heart attack – brought on by the accident."

"That's right," he agreed, "... if it was an accident." He paused slightly before continuing. "It was certainly a massive heart attack. There was no chance of saving ..."

"What do you mean – *if it was an accident?*" Selene demanded, interrupting.

"Well, for example, you said that he jumped overboard. That wouldn't be an accident, would it? I'm just saying it's too early to jump to any conclusions. That's all."

This seemed to calm Selene, who muttered something briefly under her breath and went quiet.

"Now, there's something else that has to be done. I'm afraid somebody must formally identify the body. I'm sure there are other people we could get to do it, but we always prefer relatives where possible. Do you think you'd be alright with it, Mrs Courtney?"

"I'll be OK," she said briefly, confidently.

"I'll go along with her," I volunteered.

"The Coroner has been informed, and he may ask for a post-mortem. It would be perfectly normal after an accident – or suicide. We'll have to see."

"OK," she said again.

He picked up a phone, dialled a number and was put through almost immediately. After a brief conversation, he turned back to us, "Right. Your stepfather's body is being held at the mortuary at St. Mary's Hospital, and we can go right now. Let's get it over with, eh? I'll take you."

This turned out to be just the first of many tasks in a long and busy day. The end of even the simplest of lives leaves a trail of grief — not merely emotional grief, but also matters that have to be urgently addressed; and one could never call the life of Sir James Marshall a simple one. The next couple of weeks would consist of long interviews, telephone conversations, and searches through dusty old files and the internet. Practically nothing was to be straightforward. Indeed, we were thwarted in our very first task, unable to obtain a medical certificate giving the cause of death because the Coroner had yet to decide on the need for a post-mortem. And so it went on.

Back in the apartment, I decided to give Selene a break from her wheelchair and lifted her onto the sofa. I sat beside her and put my arms around her as she snuggled up to me.

"Thanks for your support, Martin. I'm afraid it's going to get worse before it gets better. Are you sure you don't want to walk away from it all?" She looked up at me — challenging, but smiling too.

I shrugged. "I don't know. I might stick around for a day or two." She punched me then. I'm sure it was meant to be playful, but it quite hurt. Whatever power she had lost in her legs, she seemed to have gained in her arms, and I briefly pictured her struggling with her stepfather in the boat. Could she possibly have the strength?

"Ow. That hurt," I said, looking suitably pained.

"You baby," she retorted.

"You don't know your own strength," I insisted, but laughed.

"So ... where do we go from here?" she asked. I wasn't quite sure what she meant.

"Are we a couple then?" I turned the question back to her.

"It seems so," she confirmed, adding, "... if last night was anything to go by."

We had agreed to a formal alliance and kissed to seal it. For several minutes, our lips uttered no words – just kisses. I don't believe I need to describe my feelings. I had won the gold medal. I was the champion of the world – right on top of it. Between kisses, I looked at her perfect face – the tumbling golden hair, bright blue eyes, bewitching lips slightly parted in that delicious smile, and the blush of her perfectly smooth skin, the thin scar hardly visible. I couldn't believe my luck.

"You asked earlier if I fancied you. I can confirm that, Selene. I've done so from the very first time I saw you on your sun lounger. Since then, I've ached to be with you. And now I can love you – up close and personal."

As I said this, I was smothering her with kisses. Inevitably, I felt myself aroused, and my body moved inexorably on top of hers.

"Not now," she said gently, but kindly. "Later."

I pulled away slightly, unwillingly. "We have work to do," she explained. "We must get on with it. I'm not even certain we should be in this flat."

Once we had untangled ourselves, we set about dividing the work between us. It was an odd feeling, putting me back into "couples" mode. Since I had decided to take a break from work, Angie had developed the habit of setting me tasks for the day as she left for the office. She would preface many of them with the ominous words "Would you just ..." Almost invariably, such tasks would be unexpectedly complicated and involve me in several hours of dirty or fiddly work, and I came to refer to them collectively as "just jobs". To head Selene away from this practice, I volunteered for the first, and possibly most pressing, task – to find out the situation in the apartment we were now occupying.

I soon discovered how very little Selene knew about Sir James's affairs. She had no idea whether he owned the apartment or whether he, or more probably one of his companies, had rented it for the week. She pointed to a leather case in the corner of the room. "You might find something in there," she said. "We'll have to go through it anyway."

I pulled out several files, mostly named with printed labels. On the top of the pile was a thin folder with "Cowes" scribbled roughly on the front cover with a marker pen. Inside was a smart official programme of all the yacht races, ceremonial and recreational events, a few bills and return ferry tickets. But a rough scrap of paper caught my eye, containing telephoned instructions for collecting the apartment key. When I rang the listed number, it turned out to be a local firm of managing agents. Sir James's letting of the apartment had expired on the previous day, but they had heard of the accident and were happy to let us stay for one more night, after which they would need to prepare it for the next tenant.

With that agreed, "What about his car?" I asked Selene. "Didn't he drive you over here?"

"Yes, he did. I'd forgotten that", she said uncertainly. "He dropped me outside when we arrived, and we didn't use it again. There's a basement car park, but I'm not sure I'd recognise the car. In London, he drove a big Jag, but we came here in a smaller car. It's a fair size, but he used to call it his "runabout".

"Do you know where the keys are?"

"Not really, no."

I laughed. "You don't seem to know much about his affairs, do you," I said.

"No," she admitted quietly. "I don't think there were any keys in the personal effects we picked up this morning – they may have been lost at sea." She looked stumped for a moment, but then looked up, "I doubt if he'd have taken them on the boat. I think he used to empty his pockets onto the chest of drawers in his bedroom. Try there."

It was a good guess. I found a bunch of keys and down in the car park, clicking the remote soon identified a smart 5 Series BMW as his runabout. In the glove box, I found a certificate of insurance and a reasonably quick telephone call allowed me to add my name as a temporary additional driver.

"Will you be ready to leave tomorrow morning, Selene?" I asked.

"Why not," she agreed. "The police haven't asked us to stay here any longer. I'll start getting our things together."

We spent the afternoon packing, refining arrangements with the agents and answering calls offering condolences – some from friends, but mainly from business acquaintances. Among them was a call from a London firm of solicitors, offering help and announcing that they held Sir James's Will in their office and that he had appointed them as Executors and Administrators. I made a careful note of their details and told them that Selene would be in touch soon.

At one point, I escaped for an hour and walked back up the hill to collect my things. Joan was out shopping, leaving her husband in charge. He'd heard of the accident, of course, and they'd been concerned when I failed to return the previous night. Joan had packed him off down to the police station in the morning to investigate.

"They assured me it wasn't you," he said. "But where did you get to last night, if it's not a rude question?"

"It's a long story," I told him. "I spent a lot of it comforting a relative of the dead man." Well, it was true, wasn't it?

As I returned to the apartment with my tiny case of belongings, I found Selene facing a much more challenging packing job. She had crammed most of her things into one large case and was now sitting amongst piles of Sir James' clothes and other stuff. An oversize trunk lay before her, and she was wondering where to begin.

"Come on," I said. "I'll help you. Let's get it over with."

A couple of hours later, we left for dinner. I believe I have already admitted to being something of a creature of habit and, rather than take a chance on making another find, we both happily settled on the excellent table of the previous night. All was packed and we had cleared the apartment. We were ready to relax.

As we ate, we talked about many things. In all new relationships, there is much history to relate, and we hardly touched on the sad events of the previous day. At the back of my mind, I was still concerned about Selene's involvement in the death of her stepfather. I simply couldn't square some aspects. For a start, what was she doing with the man she hated? What were all the arguments about? Had I really heard the splash of Sir James falling overboard? And, if so, why was there such a delay in her calling out for help?

But I couldn't bring myself to raise it with her ... not yet, at any rate. Certainly not that evening.

The food and wine were, of course, merely appetisers for the main event, which duly took place later between the sheets. Suffice it to say that we both took our duties more seriously than in the previous night's farce and, despite an arduous day, we both summoned up enough energy for a prolonged and highly enjoyable session of lovemaking.

We awoke in the morning to find that the fine weather had broken, and it was raining hard as I drove out onto roads that were curiously unfamiliar under the leaden sky. Three hours later, Selene navigated us to a pair of high gates in a leafy Chelsea road. I got out and spoke into an intercom that was set into the surrounding brickwork. A few seconds later, the doors opened revealing a short drive to a garage, with additional parking beside it. A flight of wide stone steps led up to a tall semi-detached townhouse.

At the top of the steps, outside the open front door, an attractive middle-aged woman stood waiting for us. I realised suddenly that I had never considered the wife that Sir James had left behind. What should I call her? I started to wonder what the correct form of address was – `Milady' perhaps, or `Ma'am'?

Selene must have sensed my disquiet, for she whispered to me as we approached, "Mrs French – Jim's housekeeper." I was to discover that she and her husband occupied a half-basement service flat. In return, she cooked and kept house for Sir James living on the three floors above. Her husband acted as chauffeur and maintained both the house and garden.

"I'm so sorry Selene," she offered sympathetically. "It was a terrible shock." It must have been, I thought. Your house and jobs are now on the line. But I smiled and shook hands as Selene introduced me somewhat coyly as, "Martin Ramsay. He's an old family friend, and he's going to help me sort out Sir James's affairs." After a short pause for the explanation to sink in, she continued, "Would you please check that the guest suite is ready?"

"Of course," she said as she relieved me of my case. "If you'd like to go through to the kitchen, I've put a bite of lunch out for you. I expect you've had quite a journey."

"Yes," agreed Selene. "That's very thoughtful. Thank you."

So began our life together at the Marshall home. It was not to last very long.

Chapter 21

Selene was aware that my divorce was not yet complete and quoted this as the reason for her somewhat prudish introduction. However, I rather thought this was probably more to do with protecting her reputation, and this was later confirmed by her insistence that we should maintain propriety within the house. To accommodate Selene's disability, the dining room had been set up as her bedroom, and every morning I would be turfed out to occupy my allocated bed on the floor above. Once I had left, Selene would call down to Mrs French for assistance, and I would descend after a further half an hour or so.

When I came down that first morning, I found Selene leafing through a tattered photo album.

"Good morning, Martin," she greeted me for the benefit of Mrs French, who was by now hovering around on breakfast duty. "I've started to go through Jim's things. It seems to be down to me to organise the funeral – I can't think who else will do it. So, I need a list of all his living relatives. Allyson and Judy – the two girls from his last marriage I know well, of course. He had no children with my mother, but I know he was married once before when he was very young. They had a boy, but they didn't get on. He hated his father and, as far as I can remember, they never spoke to one another once he left school. I doubt if he'll be mentioned in Jim's Will."

"Are you expecting anything? Did he ever talk to you about it?"

"I'm not a blood relative, you know. He never mentioned anything to me but ... I don't know. I have no idea."

Mrs French came up to me. "What would you like for breakfast, Mr Ramsay? Can I cook something for you?"

I smiled at her. "No thanks, Mrs French – just some coffee, please. And I'll help myself to some cereal."

"This is him," Selene shouted. "Henry – when he was about 10. Poor little bugger. But how do I let him know that his father has died? I doubt if even Jim knew his whereabouts."

"The solicitors who telephoned," I suggested. "They're going to administer the Will. They may have a contact for him – they'll certainly want one if he's a party to it. It's worth having a word with them."

After breakfast, I decided to take the train down to Southampton to pick up my car. As I left, she was telephoning the solicitors, and so started the legal proceedings that were to lead to us being turfed out of the house, and homeless.

We soon settled into a steady routine. Selene spent most of her time wading through Sir James's private correspondence, making the funeral arrangements, talking to the solicitors and representatives of his various companies, and a host of other things that kept her skittering about the house in her wheelchair.

Whenever I was not assisting her, I was able to give some time to my impending divorce. When I telephoned Angie to find out the latest position, she sounded annoyed, and I knew I was in some sort of trouble. Having been unable to get hold of me, she had made a call to my father in Norfolk. "It was very embarrassing," she said. "And then I found he had no contact for you anyway. Where the hell have you been? Chasing after that bloody girl again?"

She had received confirmation of the date for our day in Court. Before that, I would need to gather together all the money for the agreed settlement. This was something I had sadly neglected, and I settled down to reconcile the encashed investments and to make sure the agreed figure was readily available in the Bank.

It wasn't long before the Executors invited all beneficiaries to a formal reading of Sir James's Will. Selene turned out to be the largest of the named legatees with a "nice six-figure sum", as she later reported to me. There were a handful of other legatees – either friends or close business associates, with the remainder of the estate left to the two girls – "my two gorgeous angels", as he referred to them. There was one other legacy – a final parting insult to Henry, the estranged son from his first marriage. Sir James left him the princely sum of one pound.

It is perhaps more than a little ironic that this last legacy was the only one ever to be paid in full.

The first rumble of the approaching storm sounded just a couple of days later. A letter arrived from London property agents claiming to act for the landlords of the Chelsea property in which we were living. For some reason, it had never crossed either of our minds that Sir James did not own the property, but worse was to come. The letter went on to explain that the property was leased to one of Sir James's companies, a private company, and requested information about its future following Jim's death. We passed the letter through to the solicitors, but it was already clear that our occupation of the property was precarious and likely to be short-lived.

A few days later, the solicitors confirmed the contents of the letter and went on to inform Selene that the same company also leased both the Jaguar and the BMW. Thus, we learned how the man had lived. We had already established that he held little cash in his personal bank accounts, and any wealth he possessed would lie in his investments and the companies he controlled. The Executors had appointed accountants to investigate and report on their value, and it was at this point that Selene suddenly decided to reveal to me the cause of the argument between her and her stepfather on the day of his death.

It had begun in the morning when Selene had asked him if he could let her have some money, preferably a monthly allowance. He had taken the request extremely badly, calling her an ungrateful bitch, a whore, and many other such insults. He had then ranted about the cost of his living expenses, asserting that he was bust – totally broke. He had recently been forced to refinance all his companies, and each of them was riddled with debt. No, was his firm answer. He had no money to give her.

It had flared up again on the boat when she accused him of lying. How could he live the way he did if he had no money? The row escalated to the point where they both lost control, and he moved over to her in a rage, shaking her violently. She insisted that it had taken all her strength to force him away. The recollection had clearly upset her and she was sobbing uncontrollably, her whole body shuddering with emotion. I would have liked to press her further on what happened next, but it was not the right time, and I just held her close until she gradually began to calm down.

The funeral went off without incident and the weeks passed happily enough. One morning, Mrs French and her husband received notification that the Company employing them had been dissolved, and their employment therefore terminated. Neither of us could afford to take them on, and they sadly left shortly afterwards. This left me in charge of running the house, and the quality of the meals plummeted. But at least Selene did not need to kick me out of her bed each morning.

Our relationship flourished. Whilst I began to overcome my initial amazement that Selene should accept me, she seemed to be very content with her new man, both as a companion and as a lover. In hindsight, I should perhaps have been more questioning of the willingness with which such a gorgeous creature was prepared to exchange her rich Italian aristocrat for this lowly Brit.

I didn't see Angie again until we met in Court. It was a sombre affair, but mercifully short, and we met up afterwards for a farewell drink. She had brought along a few more oddments of mine she thought I might like to keep and, as we parted for the last time, I found myself walking to the car carrying them in a cardboard box – like a sacked banker with his pathetic collection of personal belongings.

I felt real sadness as I drove back to Chelsea. Ten years of intimacy with Angie had been extinguished in as many minutes, in sharp contrast to the joyful hours of our wedding day. I decided to banish these sad thoughts, and at the same time to mark the occasion by taking Selene out to our favourite restaurant that evening.

After I had given her a full report on the day, I took her hand, "Now, what about your marriage? It's your turn next."

"You must be joking," she shouted immediately, pushing away my hand. "He's my real live piggy bank. I'm still hoping for something from Jim's estate, but I need Bob's money."

"Bob?" I queried.

"Robertson," she explained. "I always called him Bob. He was a great man, Martin – a real live wire, full of fun and a brilliant surgeon. I know, you can't see it now, can you? You've only seen him in a mental Institution."

"But he's much older than you, isn't he?"

I felt her bristle slightly at my question, and she answered indignantly, "He certainly is – more than thirty-five years older." She shrugged, and then continued, "It didn't seem important at the time. As my surgeon, of course, I owed him my life. And he's always been very good to me."

"Do you know what brought on his illness?"

She gave me an uncertain look. "I'm not a doctor, Martin," she exclaimed. "It's obviously some form of dementia, but there's something else as well. The psychiatrist gave it a long name, but I got the impression that even the experts are not entirely certain. There are lots of such conditions apparently."

"It's so sad."

"Yes, but I have no money of my own – not much anyway. I was OK when I was with Pino." She paused briefly, looking at me with a devilish smile, and then continued, "I need a man with money, Martin. And what do I get – *YOU*!"

I smiled back. "I know. You deserve better."

She leaned over and took my hand. "I'm very happy with what I've got," she purred.

"Good," I said. "But you're right, of course. I shall have to start working again before too long."

"What will you do?"

"I dunno. I'll probably go back to what I know." This set me thinking, but Chelsea was not the place to do it – much too pricey. And that led to another thought. I would need working capital, so I would have to start soon – before all my reserves were exhausted.

As I recall, it was the very next week that Selene received notice from the landlord's solicitors to quit the house. It was not unexpected – but a blow nonetheless.

"We appear to be homeless," I said. "How long have we got?"

"Twenty-eight days," she read from the letter.

"Well, we can't afford hotels for long." I paused for thought. "And my house in Italy is still a building site. Anyway, it isn't suitable for winter – it has no heating."

"You gave your father's address to the police in Cowes. Does he have room for us?"

I had considered this possibility earlier but hadn't been able to make up my mind. The spare room was big and had a double bed, but it was stuffed full of my belongings. It was far from ideal, and well short of the surroundings to which Selene was accustomed.

"I'm not sure," I said. "I'll have a word with Dad – see what he thinks."

I should never have doubted my father. "Of course, my boy," was his immediate reaction, and he followed this up with a practical suggestion. "The room's full of your clobber, you know ..."

"I know," I interrupted. "And I shall be bringing some more," and then added, "and Selene will have a load of her own."

"I can imagine," my father said. "I was just about to say, I have a farmer friend who's set up a small trading estate from some of his outbuildings. He has some storage units and I'm sure we can get some space at a reasonable rate. I suggest we move all the stuff you're not likely to be using into it. And if you do find you need something, it's very close by."

"That sounds great, Dad. Thanks a lot."

Before we headed for Norfolk, however, I was to witness a most disconcerting outburst from Selene. The post arrived one morning as we were having breakfast, and she started reading a letter from the solicitors. "It's an interim report on Jim's estate," she announced. I watched as her eyes moved down over the text, and could see the muscles in her neck tighten as her anger grew.

"*The bastard*," she exploded finally. After a few moments of ominous silence, she said quietly – but full of pent-up anger, "Get me a drink, Martin."

"It's only nine in the morning, darling ..."

"Get me a fucking drink," she demanded loudly and shot me a glance that resembled hatred. This shook me, and I hurriedly poured her a stiff vodka and tonic.

She flung the letter at me. "The ungrateful bastard," she continued her rant. "After all I've done for the revolting man."

I picked up the letter and started to read it. "Don't bother," she spat at me. "It just says I'll get nothing."

I skipped to the last paragraph.

'With all this in mind, it is most unlikely that the estate will amount to a positive figure. It will be several months before the accountants reconcile the assets with all the liabilities, and only then will the legacies be apportioned pro rata. At this stage, however, I regret to have to inform you that if any legacy does become payable, it is most unlikely to be more than a nominal figure.'

"That's a shame," I said.

She looked at me as if I was mad, saying nothing for a few moments – just staring. Then she suddenly picked up the teapot, and I prepared to duck as she looked to throw it at me. At the last moment, she aimed at the wall, smashing it with shards of china and tea bags flying in all directions.

I shot up from the table. "Selene," I shouted.

She showed no sign of contrition and followed the teapot with her cereal bowl shouting at the top of her voice, "You don't fucking understand. I deserve that money. I earned it. You have no idea what I have had to do for it."

"Calm down," I said as gently as I could manage. I desperately wanted her to stop, not because I felt in any danger, but because for the very first time, I found her unattractive. She could never look ugly, but her furious, snarling face was unsightly – bordering on grotesque.

Very gradually, her anger subsided and she sat back panting from her exertions. Her face slowly relaxed until she once again became recognisable as the girl of my dreams. But I could think of nothing to break down the wall of silence, until she finally said quietly, "I'm sorry, Martin. I needed that money."

I went around the table and wrapped my arms around her. The episode was over.

And so too was our time in Chelsea. A couple of weeks later, we were heading for Norfolk and a very different lifestyle.

Chapter 22

Once we had redistributed our possessions as my father had suggested, our life settled into a comfortable routine, although we were both aware that it could only be temporary. My father seemed to treat Selene rather warily from the outset, but his wife immediately took her under her wing. Dad had always appreciated a beautiful woman – he had married three of them – and I was somewhat unsettled by his coolness towards her. Could it possibly have been some old man's jealousy of his son's good fortune? I think it is more likely that he spotted some flaw in her character, or maybe it was simply that his many years had taught him that nothing could be that perfect.

Before the winter began to close in, he and I would take the boat along the coast, sometimes trying a little fishing. On one such occasion, I plucked up courage, "What do you think of Selene, Dad?"

No sooner had I uttered the words, than I regretted them and felt nervous about his response. I also felt it was perhaps an unfair question, and quickly added, "That's an unreasonable question, Dad. You don't have to answer it."

"No," he replied. "I'll answer. But why do you ask? Have I been unfriendly towards her?"

"No. No," I assured him swiftly. "Not unfriendly. Quite the reverse. I just feel some ... wariness. That's all."

My father thought for a while. "As you know, I was a classics scholar, Martin. I studied quite a bit of Greek mythology, and remember that Selene was a goddess."

That shook me. I was sure I had never mentioned to him that I had secretly appointed her as my personal deity. But he continued almost immediately, "Yup. She was a moon goddess – the personification of the moon itself. She was beautiful and sensuous, but she had many lovers, both mortals and Gods – including Zeus himself, I believe."

"Really," was all I could manage, not certain where he was going.

"Ouf, that's not fair. What's in a name? I'm sure she's fine. She's certainly very beautiful. You're a lucky man."

And that was as far as I got. He would elaborate no further. Maybe he had some second sense – one that I had failed to inherit.

As autumn stuttered imperceptibly into winter, so did Selene's disposition begin to change. She was unaccustomed to the shackles of rural life, particularly in a season she considered was designed for winter sports or travel to warm tropical places. We were comfortable enough in the sanctuary of my father's house, but their friends were necessarily of a different generation, and she began to miss her considerable circle, few of whom made the journey to Wells – preferring the slopes of

Saint Moritz. Although skiing itself was denied to her, of course, Selene missed her usual seasonal buzz of après-ski entertainment.

Winter can be severe in this little nib of England, and it wasn't long before we had to haul the boat ashore for the season. This left little more than walks for recreation, and I must have covered nearly every inch of the area, either cross-country with my father or pushing Selene around the roads and tracks. Even before Christmas, I too was becoming restless from the enforced inactivity and decided to make efforts to resume work in the world of property development. I found the local scene very sluggish, however, and each time I seemed close to an opportunity, I found myself thwarted by a cartel of local developers.

Whilst these efforts may have been diverting for me, they left Selene with little to entertain her. She was still my goddess. I had explored every inch of her now, and I still worshipped every single one. Both day and night, we were still enjoying each other's company. But the intensity of the honeymoon period was beginning to shine a little less brightly. Some seemingly innocuous disagreements led to furious outbursts by Selene. I soon learned to back away from these at the earliest opportunity, but her anger would become almost unstoppable, with the intensity increasing until she was screaming like a banshee and bashing into me violently with her wheelchair. I remembered Giovanni recounting this to me, but I was surprised at the skill with which she had learned to do it, and how much it would hurt.

Embarrassingly, my father and Stephanie witnessed a number of these episodes. After one particularly noisy tantrum, my father took me aside. "She likes her own way, your Selene, doesn't she?" he began. "And what a temper – reminds me of my second wife." I could see what he meant, and this remark shook me. I remembered the terrible atmosphere that accompanied the final death throes of that relationship, and I did not want us to end up like that.

Even today, I am unsure how we managed to survive those many days before the first small signs of an English spring encouraged us to pack our bags for Italy. I recall that we did spend a good deal of the time in the bedroom. The rest remains a blurred collage of freezing hands and feet after walks, mindless hours of television, pouring vodka and tonics for Selene and endless meals prepared with remarkable stoicism by Stephanie.

But I do recall with great clarity the evening I received yet another warning of my involvement with Selene. And it came from a most unexpected source.

One welcome diversion turned out to be the local pub. An enterprising landlord put on a variety of entertainments from quizzes to live music of all sorts, and it was here that we managed to prise open a small crack into the sturdy barricades erected by the younger set of Wells inhabitants. It was a somewhat parochial mix of young marrieds and singles, most of whom had known each other all their lives. Maybe it was simply the novelty of some new blood, but a number of them took us under their wing and invited us to their parties. One such had been arranged to celebrate April Fool's Day.

I knew that there was considerable money in the area, but both of us were surprised by the sheer size of the mansion to which we were ushered by the dozens of balloons that festooned the entrance gates. The party was already in full swing, with a live group playing in the vast main living room. I settled Selene in a chair at the edge of the dancing throng and went in search of some drinks.

"I'm not driving," she shouted after me. These words contained two coded messages. The first was to ensure that her vodka and tonics were of generous strength and length. The corollary was that driving safely was my responsibility, and demanded that I remained sober. Throughout the evening, I would add only a splash of gin to a tumbler of tonic, and try to imagine that it was the same drink that my father mixed for me each evening before dinner.

The large country kitchen was awash with catering staff preparing a variety of party foods, and the adjacent dining area had been set up as the bar for the evening. I ran into George, an occasional member of our quiz team, and we chatted as our drinks were poured. We had not seen much of him of late, and he explained that he had broken up with his girlfriend. He tried to put a brave face on it, but I could see he was upset and I commiserated.

"George, I'm so sorry. I haven't known you that long, but you two seemed to be such a ... well, such a couple. We always thought you'd be the next to get married."

"I thought so too, Martin. It was quite a shock. I guess she just found some guy she liked a bit better."

"Is it someone I might know?"

"No. I don't know him either – someone from work."

"I'm so sorry," I repeated. "My marriage broke up last year, so I know how you must feel."

As we parted with our drinks, he offered prophetically, "Watch out, Martin, there's a lot of it about. And Selene's a lovely girl."

I smiled as we went our separate ways, but I hurried to get the vodka to Selene before any delay upset her. I found her surrounded by three men, who parted rather sheepishly as I forced my arm through to get the drink to her. She seemed to be having a good time, no doubt working her magic with the audience, so I decided to circulate for a while.

The party had spread throughout the whole of the ground floor, a bewildering series of rooms. For the hardier souls, it extended outside onto the terrace where I spotted George and some other friends and went to join them. It was a bit chilly, but a couple of patio heaters rendered it tolerable. My first drink always disappears very quickly at parties and in no time, I was replenishing it, along with other empties. On my way back, I checked on Selene who now had a sizeable crowd around her. She was doing just fine, I decided and carried on outside.

One or two strangers had joined our little group, and I got talking to Rachel. She was a tall, attractive, dark-haired girl who reminded me of Julie, the girl I had met in Cowes – not by her looks, but more by her mannerisms and demeanour. She oozed confidence, but with the same attractive feminine shades that I had found in Julie.

After a while, Rachel announced that she was feeling cold and the two of us went inside to the bar. I was greatly relieved when she turned down my offer to take her to the dance floor. I can jog around aimlessly if pressed, but it is not one of my greatest accomplishments. Fortunately, she protested that it was "all too noisy in there", and we found a place to talk in what seemed to be the library.

It was a lively conversation as others joined us, sheltering either from the cold outside or from the bedlam in the main room. The best part of two hours passed very quickly, punctuated every so often by visits to the bar. Whenever it was my turn, I would look in on Selene who continued to attract a crowd and dismissed any need for my attention with a cheery wave. I have purposely not dwelt on the extra demands placed on living with someone confined to a wheelchair. It can well be imagined how much it affects daily life – morning, noon and even during the night. Toilet calls are but one of the constant demands, but I knew better than to interrupt Selene's current flow with any "Do you need the toilet?" enquiry. She would have no hesitation in requesting help as the moment required.

It was well after one in the morning before our little party began to break up. The main room was still in full swing, and I took Rachel in to introduce her to Selene. She was not where I had seated her and I could see no sign of her anywhere in the room. We had left her wheelchair under the stairs in the hall, but there was no sign of that either. Asking around elicited nothing more than a series of shaking heads until one girl said, "I think I saw a wheelchair being pushed into a room over there."

She waved her hands lazily at the far end of the hall, but her slurred speech failed to instil any great confidence in her suggestion. Nevertheless, Rachel and I went over to explore a couple of doors in the area she had indicated. The first turned out to be an empty cloakroom, but the other was locked, or so it seemed at first. But then I spotted a button glowing at the side and realised it was an elevator - another surprise in this most surprising house. I pressed the button and the door whispered open.

Upstairs, it re-opened onto a large landing, where a bathroom immediately opposite stood with its door open. A guest, clearly the worse for wear, was kneeling bent over the toilet making noises that began to turn our stomachs, and we swiftly turned into the wide corridor that led off to the right. As we did so, a door further along it opened and a wheelchair began to emerge. I was not surprised a moment later to see that it was holding Selene, but the young man pushing her was something of a shock – he can have been little more than half her age. Both Rachel and I stopped in our tracks as they approached. It could have been my imagination, but I thought the two of them looked very sheepish – particularly the young man. And it didn't help that Rachel was staring at me, wondering how I would react.

"I needed the bathroom," Selene explained simply as we stepped aside to let them through to the lift. Both Rachel and I remained speechless, just staring at them as they passed. There would not be sufficient room for all of us in the small lift, so we took the stairs and I bit my lip and said nothing until we had caught up with them in the hall. Having introduced the girls, I turned to the young man, "I'm sorry I don't know your name."

"Mark," he said simply, and stood there – flushed, looking like an idiot, but I had already decided that this was neither the time nor the place for a confrontation. Selene was also flushed, but also extremely giggly, and I put it all down to the quantity of vodka she must have drunk during the evening. She started quizzing Rachel about herself, and Mark slowly began to back away from the group. Eventually, muttering some almost inaudible words of excuse, he turned and almost ran towards the crowded dance floor.

The girls were now deep in conversation, and I slipped away quietly. They were too involved to notice that we were right by the hall's vacant toilet and I leapt up the stairs again, two at a time. I did need the toilet, but first I went to the room from which the two had emerged. My fears were confirmed as soon as I entered. It was no bathroom, but a bedroom. I stood in the open doorway for several seconds, checking all the details of the room and then staring at nothing in particular, my mind racing.

Whoever had been sick in the bathroom had made a reasonable job of cleaning up the mess, but I stood warily as I relieved myself of a good portion of the evening's refreshments. The two girls were still chattering excitedly as I slowly descended the stairs to join them.

With George as a singleton now, there was room for new blood in our quiz team, and I eventually managed to secure a brief gap in their conversation. "Rachel, why don't you join us next Wednesday at the pub quiz?" I suggested.

"Yes," she said guardedly. "Maybe – I'll see."

I turned to Selene. "Come on. You're in your chair now. I think it's time we were going."

"Oh no, darling," she began, her speech more than a little slurred. "It's early yet. Let's stay a bit longer."

Was she trying to put off the moment we would be alone? And the "darling" had tripped off her lips a bit too readily.

"No. Come on, Selene. It's half past one – and I'm tired."

You may well imagine the awkward drive home. She had drunk far too much for me to voice my suspicions. Her reaction would be unpredictable, which would be highly dangerous with me at the wheel. And I felt no different in the house with my father and Stephanie asleep. Whatever her reaction, it was likely to be noisy.

It was a struggle to get Selene into bed, but she was asleep as soon as her head touched the pillow, with her breathing settling immediately into the softly flickering pattern that I knew so well. I too was tired, and the alcohol helped me to a fitful sleep. In waking moments, the incident played repeatedly in my mind, but I could only see one likely scenario. How should I react? Should I quietly walk away? Coming on top of all the warnings and subsequent suspicions, this was my immediate reaction. A simple yellow card would surely be insufficient for such a betrayal.

The morning promised much, with the sun heralding a glorious spring day. But my heart was heavy, and my mind was full of the conflict to come. Breakfast passed amicably enough as we recounted the events of the evening and the fabulous house where the party was held. It turned out that my father knew of the house, but our hosts only by reputation. This was the morning for their weekly expedition to a supermarket in Fakenham, and I shooed them out as soon as we had finished, promising to clear away breakfast. I could put the moment off no longer.

As I put away the last of the things, I turned and leant back against the granite worktop. "Tell me about last night," I started. "Tell me what you were doing upstairs with that young lad."

She retained a smile and pulled a rebuking face, with a finger wagging at me. "Are we a jealous little boy?" she accused.

In hindsight, perhaps I should have pulled away at this point. I knew well that my powers of slinging vitriol were no match for those of Selene, and her opening show of defiance had all the hallmarks of the calm before a violent storm. But I simply had to know.

"Tell me what you got up to," I demanded sternly.

The smile disappeared from her face. "I told you, I needed the loo," she said flatly, challenging any dispute.

"No, Selene. It may have started that way, but the room from which he wheeled you was not a bathroom – it was a bedroom. I saw where you had come from, and I checked."

She was getting angry now. "*You checked ...*" she screamed. "I used the en suite toilet."

"I checked that too. There was no en suite." She had lost all the colour in her cheeks, as I pressed again, "And the bedding was all rucked up. Someone had been lying on it."

I could see that the storm was about to break. "You fucker," she spat. "You chase me round the world. You tell me you love me. But now don't trust me. You check up on me. You're the same as all the other men. You are jealous ... and possessive."

She paused briefly to catch her breath, but she was not finished. "Well, I warn you, Martin. I'm not the girl for you. We have no future together." And she started to wheel herself towards the door.

"Stay where you are," I barked, and to my amazement, she did.

"I want to know what you got up to with Mark – how far you went."

"All the way, Martin," she shouted. "All the fucking way, and it was a lot better than the sex I've been getting here lately."

My face must have been a picture, but not an attractive one. She knew precisely how best to hurt a man, and had hit me unerringly below the belt. I had expected her to continue with denials, and the force of her admission took me by surprise. I stood silent for a moment, mouth open.

"Ha," she exploded triumphantly and turned the chair once more to leave.

As she did so, I said quietly, "How could you, Selene?"

She turned back. "*How could I?* How could I? It was easy. You can't tell me what to do and what not to do. You don't own me, you pathetic little man. Just bugger off." Turning, she wheeled herself at great speed out of the room.

I stood still, staring at the space where the wheelchair had stood. Suddenly, my life had become simpler. She had taken out of my hands the decision I had been struggling with for some time. Not only had she added her warning to the list of many others, but she had also offered a solution. We had no future together – we were through.

I went for a long walk with my father that afternoon.

"Selene and I – we're splitting up," I told him when a lull appeared in our conversation.

I hadn't meant to catch him unawares, but it shook him. "I'm so sorry son," he said. "Stephi will be very upset."

No one will be more upset than me," I retorted. "I've invested a lot of time in her – and money." That sounded a trifle mercenary I thought, and added, "Anyway, the silly part about it is ... I believe I'm still in love with her."

My father said nothing but put his arm around my shoulder and gave me a gentle hug. It was over almost immediately, but it was the warmest physical sign of affection I could remember receiving from him since babyhood. I was touched and looked up at him and smiled in thanks.

I had decided not to tell either of them about her recent indiscretion – it would unnecessarily turn them against her. I had to find another reason for the breakup.

"It's just ... well, this may sound a bit ridiculous, but I'm not sure she's safe to be with. One of her previous men warned me about her. He told me about her violent outbursts – you've seen some of the milder ones yourself. Well, he nearly died at her hands ..."

"Good grief man," my father interrupted.

"She'd cut his leg – severed some arteries. He said it was an accident, and I'm sure it probably was. But equally certainly, it was the result of one of her furious tantrums. I've seen too many of them now. I simply can't control her."

"I can't say I'm too surprised," my father said. "We've noticed her mood swings. I think you're probably well out of it, son."

That evening, Selene joined us for dinner and was a changed person. I assumed that my father would have relayed our conversation to Stephanie, and they must both have been as confused as I was. She acted as if nothing had happened, laughing and joking, and narrating some of the stories she had heard the previous night. In the end, we all joined in with some forced good cheer that was so far preferable to the gloomy silence we had all anticipated.

But inevitably bedtime arrived and, with no alternative sleeping arrangements available, I wheeled Selene into our room for what I guessed might well be the last time. Even before I had the chance to move her onto the bed, she grabbed hold of me and began weeping.

"I'm so sorry darling," she began. "Please forgive me. I was stupid. I was drunk."

She must have recognised that I was not in any mood for forgiveness, and continued amid heaving bouts of tears, "Oh, I can't even forgive myself. Why should you forgive me? But please, darling, please, I don't want to lose you ..."

She was leaning forward in her chair, holding both my hands, almost incoherent by now, alternately crying and begging forgiveness.

Even as I began to respond, tentatively at first accepting and then caressing her hands, I knew I should be resisting. But I am only human, and I had admitted to still loving the girl only a few short hours earlier. How could I not but melt? I can hardly believe it now, but within a few minutes, I was sweeping her up in my arms and taking her to bed. Given the circumstances, it was a most extraordinary experience.

Understandably, it was a very confused father who waved us goodbye a few days later as we left on the long journey to Lombardy.

Chapter 23

I had forgotten that Selene had only visited the Italian house in one of my dreams. As we entered, its inadequacies were immediately apparent. It was so small and felt cold with the early spring sun unable yet to banish the winter's chill. Selene was accustomed to much grander surroundings, but somehow that failed to concern me, and I realised very quickly that whatever she felt about it mattered very little. The notion came as quite a shock to me. I didn't care.

This led to a re-evaluation of our relationship. She still possessed the same beautiful face, body, laugh, and mannerisms – all the things I had found so attractive. And yet, none of it meant quite so much to me now. The chase was over, and I had achieved my twin goals. But so too was our honeymoon over, and I felt that the last of our days together was rapidly approaching.

"What a great place," I heard her say, but the words did not match the eyes as they roamed around the unfinished ceiling and yet undecorated walls.

"Well," I said. "As you can see, there's still a hell of a lot to do."

I settled down to this work the next day. Up to now, I had applied a rather scattergun approach, with the result that large areas of unfinished work were starkly conspicuous, both on the outside and in every room. It could be rainy at this time of year, so I decided to leave the external work for the summer. As far as possible, I would concentrate on completing one room at a time – starting with the kitchen and dining area. This was self-contained, with direct access to the outside, and would free up the remaining space for Selene.

The weather was not kind to us, and it was barely more than a week before the inevitable began. "Martin, can't we go off somewhere today," Selene implored as we finished breakfast. "I'm bored."

"I know, darling. I told you this might not be a good idea," I sighed. It was little more than a building site, but it was our only home. A further problem was the confined space, which made it difficult for Selene to wheel herself around in her chair. Unable to help me, except for making the occasional cup of tea, she must have felt useless, her life hopelessly confined.

"Where would you like to go?"

She thought for a moment. "Rome would be nice. I have some friends there."

"Oh, Selene. That's about the most expensive place in Europe. You know I simply don't have the money for that sort of thing."

"I've got some money," she asserted, but then added quietly, "I know. Don't worry. I was only joking. Let's just have a day out in Bergamo. We need to look for some furniture for this place – a settee for a start."

I thought for a moment. "OK," I agreed reluctantly. When I am in the middle of a job, I find interruptions most unwelcome, but I owed her some time. I understood how she felt.

In the event, it might have been cheaper to take her to Rome. She insisted on kitting out the living room with an entire suite and then fell for an oak table and chairs for the dining area. I would certainly need such furniture, but in due time – when the rooms were ready to receive them. I did approve of her choices, however, and felt unable to refuse her, and ordered them for delivery in a few weeks. It was an enjoyable day out, and I realised that I would have to build in such days of leisure and rest.

A couple of days later, Selene wheeled herself up to me as I was fitting a cupboard in a corner of the kitchen.

"I've just had a great idea," she said excitedly. "Whilst you're working on your own house, we'd be much more comfortable in the House in the Lake. I'm sure it'll be free at this time of year, so I just have to phone Justin. What do you think?"

"Yes ... what a good idea. I don't know why we didn't think of it before. Give him a ring."

A quarter of an hour later, we were planning the move, which then took the remainder of the day. The first call was to the local mini-supermarket, which held the keys. Getting Selene into the small boat was even more difficult than the last occasion in Cowes, but she talked me through her well-practised method and we managed to land her safely. When I opened up the house, it appeared to be just as I had left it to Inspector Grimaldi the best part of a year earlier.

Selene was right, and we were able to make ourselves much more comfortable. Justin had allowed us to reserve the house for the next two months, and we settled ourselves into a daily routine. After breakfast, I would take the boat and work on the house for the day. In the evenings, we would enjoy whatever Selene had managed to put together for a meal, and then perhaps watch some Italian television or a film on DVD, or sometimes play a game of Scrabble. Later, in the bedroom, Selene generally took charge. She was the tigress she had always been, and I was happy to play along.

The weather gradually improved, and Selene was able to wheel herself down to the lower terrace. She loved to soak up whatever sun was going. The pool had been in a parlous state when we arrived, full of branches and leaves that had turned the water an unappetising brown. One day, presumably at the behest of Justin or his agent, a swarthy young Italian appeared and spent most of the day emptying, cleaning and re-filling it. He announced he would be servicing it a couple of times each month and showed me how I should carry out daily maintenance.

Summer was beckoning, and with a pile of books and magazines to read in the ever-warming sun, I felt that Selene was becoming more content.

But within a fortnight, she was again itching to move on.

"Capri," she announced one evening. "I often go there in the spring. I have a friend who has a villa there – or rather, her parents do. They've often told me I would always be welcome."

"Selene – not again. We've been over this before. I don't move in those sorts of circles. I'd be a fish out of water, uncomfortable. Anyway, we'd need money for that."

"Don't be such a fucking wimp, Martin," she said testily. "You have some money. So do I – and I can get some more. I only have to ask Justin."

"Oh come on, Selene. You can't go on taking money from your poor old husband. It isn't fair."

I could see she was beginning to get annoyed now. "*Fair?* What's not fair? He got full value from me, for Chrissake. Nearly five fucking years ..."

I hated the swearing she used when she was angry, and she knew it. But I simply said quietly, "Well, you married him."

"Yes. I did ... but why do you think I married him?

I didn't like the way the conversation was going. "Well," I suggested haltingly. "I ... I suppose you fell in love with him."

"Tch, you've gotta be joking. He was more than twice my age. Oh, I was fond of him. And I was very grateful – he did a great job on me. And he was always kind and generous." She stopped for a moment.

"I don't get it," I said apprehensively.

"What don't you get? You're really thick sometimes, Martin."

She seemed to go into a trance for a moment or two before she continued, "Do you think life's been easy for me? Think about it. I never knew my father. My mother brought me up as a single child – probably spoilt me rotten. And then, when she married my wretched stepfather, I could want for nothing. He was rich or seemed to be then, and we moved around in all the privileged circles. She died when I was still young, and I got married to escape Jim's clutches. That marriage ended with the crash, and when I came round, Bob's face was the first I saw. He carried out all the surgery and looked after me during the many months I spent in the hospital. This gave me lots of time to think, and I soon realised my precarious position. I doubted whether my young husband would have left a Will, but I knew there was no money there anyway. I would be practically penniless, tied to a wheelchair, and with no skills with which to earn a living." She paused briefly.

"Well, I did have one skill. And soon after I left the hospital, when he asked me to marry him, I accepted."

"Just for his money ... "I said, amazed and saddened at the same time.

"Don't you come all holier than thou," she snapped, her anger rising again. "You've never been in that position. You have no idea what it's like."

"No. But that's because I was brought up properly – complete with morals ..."

I should not have said this. I realise it now. But I had judged that the genie was out of the bottle, and I might as well follow it to wherever it would lead.

"Don't you throw your fucking morals at me, you stupid little boy," she was well on her way now. I'd seen it before and my anxiety was rising. "Yes, I've lived off men all my adult life. And look what I've ended up with - YOU. You're useless at keeping me happy – in any way. You can't afford me, and you're useless in bed. Pino had loads of money ... and he was great in the sack."

I started to walk away then.

"Don't you turn your back on me, you dickhead." With great speed and skill, she spun her chair and wheeled it around to confront me, red in the face, eyes blazing.

I've seen it in films – oilmen use dynamite to blow out wildcat wellhead fires, starving them of air. At that moment, I needed a stick of their dynamite to extract some of the oxygen from her fury.

"What about your stepfather then? What about Jim? Did you drown him when he refused to give you the money you were demanding?"

The effect was certainly explosive. She wheeled herself backwards a foot or so. "What the fuck are you talking about?" she demanded.

"On the boat. Did you push him overboard?"

"How the hell do you think I could do that? I was immobile – in a chair, and he was a big man."

She paused for a moment, apparently recalling the scene, and then continued in a softer, more conciliatory tone, "We had a furious row – one we'd started earlier. He was beside himself and came up to me, shouting in my face. I did push him away and ... I saw him stumble. I don't know whether he tripped or jumped. I don't know."

"I know how strong your arms are. I don't know whether to believe you or not."

She said nothing, so I continued, "However it happened, you didn't raise the alarm immediately, did you? You left it for several minutes to make sure he couldn't be rescued."

"He was a foul man," she spat her anger once again taking hold. "He deserved to die. He cheated me of my money."

"How cheated you? As you once reminded me, you're no blood relative. You had no entitlement to anything. Anyway, he was broke. He didn't have any money to give you."

"And that's what the quarrel in the boat was about. He told me he hadn't any money, and couldn't give me any. I didn't believe him – the way he lived, it didn't ring true. He promised me, and I'd earned it."

"How had you earned it? What are you talking about?" As I said this, I felt a sinking feeling in the pit of my stomach.

"How do you think, you stupid fucker? Haven't you been listening? Just wake up to the world."

Aghast, I reeled backwards. "You were screwing him, weren't you? That revolting pack of lard ... the man you loathed. You sold your body to him."

"Where could I turn to when I left Pino," she shouted defiantly. "He'd forced himself on me when I was a young teenager, so I knew what to expect. It was almost like coming home ..."

Her words had silenced me, and for several seconds I simply stared at her, perhaps hoping to see some small sign of remorse. But all that was on offer was a stony look of continued defiance.

"You disgust me," I said forcefully, unable to withhold an accompanying look of scorn. Immediately, I pushed my way past her and started out of the room.

"Where do you think you're going? Come back here," she shrieked and started wheeling herself after me.

I managed to reach the spare room – the one I had slept in that first night, rushed in and locked the door. She was soon hammering on it, screeching obscenities. The noise got louder as she crashed the wheelchair into the door, and I felt real fear as I saw the hinges begin to give. But the house had been expensively built and the quality woodwork withstood the battering. After a while, her efforts became increasingly feeble and her screams turned to uncontrollable tears. It was some time before these subsided into sobs until I heard her go into our bedroom and shut the door.

I began to relax physically but, as I threw myself onto the bed, my head was still spinning. I could hardly believe what I had heard, yet I knew it was true. Uninvited and unwelcome, visions of the brutish man making love to my one-time goddess sickened me to the core. I could not put them out of my mind and lay panting with emotion.

Much passed through my mind over the next several minutes. What sort of monster was she? Certainly, her childhood had been difficult. She never knew her father and lost her mother at an early age. Then she had then been horribly abused by her stepfather and in desperation had married the first man that came along. Together with a severely unfunded taste for the high life, this had shaped her attitude toward men. She loved them, and she hated them. With the physical attributes that nature had lavished upon her, she had no difficulty in capturing the heart of any man she pleased. But his principal job was to finance her extravagant lifestyle, and when they failed, she would simply spit them out, just as Justin had described. Although there were probably others, I knew the fate of a number of her men and in each case, she was somehow involved in their fall. Her first husband was dead, her second languishing in a mental institution. Her stepfather too was now also dead, and the extent of her hand in it remained uncertain. Her Italian lover had barely escaped with his life but with a most vicious wound.

One thing was clear to me, I needed to get away – and fast. I had no wish to be near her for another minute. But my trust in her had evaporated to such a degree that I had visions of her waiting to pounce on the other side of the door, knife in hand, so I lay back in an effort to calm my mind and plan my escape.

I would not have thought it possible, but I managed to relax to the point of sleep. It cannot have been long – two or three hours perhaps before I awoke with a start. The light was still on and I immediately got up and dressed. Checking that I had all my essential possessions, I happily recalled that my passport was safely back in my house. Quietly, I eased open the window and crawled through, dropping gently onto the path, and made my way down to the boat that was tied up at the jetty. No sound came from the house as I silently paddled my way out into the lake.

It was an eerie journey. Occasional light clouds scudded across a blood-red moon that flirted with the tree line above the surrounding hills. Its unusual light painted the landscape in unworldly hues, but I had no difficulty finding my way to the little beach from where my year's adventure had begun. I pulled the boat up from the water and drove the car home.

As the road climbed, so the blood-drenched moon invaded more of my view, and I wonder now if the terrible events that followed were perhaps merely fantasies as my unconscious mind dredged up ancient biblical warnings that such lunar eclipses presage some awful disaster.

But I had no time for such thoughts on that night. Stripping off my clothes, I got into bed, not for one moment expecting to sleep. I was emotionally drained, however, and once again managed to fall into a deep and long slumber.

Increasingly over the next few days, I found myself comforted by a feeling of closure. For some weeks, I had been expecting the breakdown of our relationship, almost as if waiting for such an outburst. Now it had finally happened, and I was relieved to be free.

I threw myself enthusiastically into work on the house. Inevitably, my thoughts occasionally returned to Selene, but they were very different from those of twelve months earlier. I found myself fearful of how she might act. Would she turn up, weapon in hand, bent on vengeance? It was illogical, of course. She would need considerable help, but the mind plays odd tricks, that sometimes defy simple logic.

But on the third day, as I was putting the finishing touches to the kitchen, some nagging doubts began to creep into my mind – pangs of conscience about the way I had left her. I tried to visualise her probable moves. I knew that she could get herself onto the bed, even if only partially undressed, and get up again the following day. She had her phone, and some money from Justin, and I convinced myself that she would be able to get help.

But, every so often, I was beset by niggling uncertainties. Her uncomplaining self-reliance had always impressed me, but she was nevertheless in need of constant care. What would happen, for example, if her mobile failed to work? Even if she were able to drag herself down to the jetty, she couldn't swim and I had taken the only boat on the island. She would be marooned, and may eventually starve to death. At first, the strength of my disaffection led me to ignore thoughts of any rescue, but as the doubts continued into the evening, I realised I would have to visit the island once again to establish that she was safe.

I opened a bottle of whisky and settled back on the sofa to plan my rescue mission. As I drank, I mulled over the revelations that had put the finishing touches to my already faltering infatuation. I was a free man.

But I also realised that I did have this one last duty call to make. The alcohol went down too easily that night. I tried to keep my mind on my plan for the next day, but random episodes from my year of passion kept interrupting it until I eventually gave up and took my exhausted body to bed.

Chapter 24

It was raining heavily when I awoke, and I decided to put off my journey until the afternoon. I would need to leave the boat on the island, so I packed my swimsuit in a stout plastic bag before driving down to the lake. A watery sun had reappeared by the time I was once again climbing the path up to the house. Over time, we had become accustomed to using the patio doors almost exclusively, and I automatically worked my way around to the rear terrace.

I was surprised to find one of the patio doors open and I hovered for a moment at the opening, uncertain of what to expect. I was just about to enter when I heard a moan from inside – a woman's moan. I stopped in my tracks and listened intently. After a short break came another cry, lingering longer before tailing off and almost immediately followed by a deep groan from a man. I knew instantly that I had stumbled on a couple having sex.

I thought I was immune to any further surprises from Selene and I just stood there, stunned. I assumed it would be Selene, but who was the man – that Italian hunk who cleaned the pool? Was she simply filling a spare half hour for him, his work thwarted by the weather? Surely not, I thought, but I had to find out. Who had she found to fill my role so seamlessly?

I felt sick and needed time to think. My mouth felt as dry as the desert and I wandered through to the kitchen in a daze. After gulping down two large glasses of water, I stood with my head bent and my hands gripping the taps, somehow expecting guidance from the bottom of the sink. What action should I take?

After several moments, from the very corner of my eye, I spotted a large carving knife lying on the draining board. Briefly, I wondered whether this was the knife that Selene had wielded at the start of my great adventure. It glinted in the sun that now streamed through the window, inviting me to pick it up. The growing sounds of passion from the bedroom had prised open a small hatch somewhere at the back of my brain, spilling out increasing waves of anger, and my hand involuntarily moved towards the handle. I hesitated . . . and then pulled it away.

But my resolve had been steeled, and I marched purposely through the sitting room and tugged open the bedroom door. Their reactions were immediate. Selene peered around the man's left shoulder as he lay on her with a look of surprise, mixed with fear. Without turning his head, the man leant back to get hold of the sheet which barely covered his legs and pulled it up over his body and head. But it was all too late. I needed no second look as the thick mat of black hair covering the man's back told me instantly the identity of Selene's new lover. He rolled off the far side of the bed leaving Selene naked and unable to move. I ignored her screams and ran around the bed to where he was desperately trying to hide. Yanking away the sheet, my conclusion was immediately confirmed . . . it was her Italian Barone, Guiseppi Morandi. She must have called him for help and was now rewarding his prompt rescue in the way she best knew.

His reaction was unexpected, but instant. Without attempting to cover his nakedness, he stood up and stood with legs set wide apart, shameless and grinning. "I warned you, young man," he yelled. "Selene is not the girl for you. You must know you're out of your depth, man."

This arrogant remark merely added to my fury. I find it difficult to explain, or even to understand, the degree of rage that now overcame me. I had provocation, certainly, but I am normally reasonably composed. I can only assume that each one of us has a point at which our natural temperament is strained to breaking point, and I had reached mine. My head thumped, my heart raced, and I saw everything around me through a dense red haze.

I rushed from the room and picked up the knife I had rejected only a moment earlier. As I re-entered the bedroom, Guiseppi was standing beside the bed, still naked. But his smile disappeared as he spotted the blade in my hand, and he started towards me. This was a powerful and fit man, but my rage had given me the strength of a superhuman and I lunged at his body as he closed. With sickening ease, the steel pierced the skin and continued deep into his ribcage where it must have torn into his heart, for Guiseppi immediately collapsed onto the bed, holding his chest. He looked down, seemingly puzzled, as blood began to seep through his fingers. But before long, he was choking up huge gouts.

It had all happened in a trice, and for several seconds, I simply stared at him as he steadily continued to bleed out. Meanwhile, Selene's screams had become increasingly hysterical, and I turned my attention to her. She was a fearful sight, with wild eyes and a face streaked with mascara. I threw down the knife, but the screaming continued. I shouted at her to stop, but her shrieks became louder still . . . I simply had to stop them.

Picking up a pillow, I forced it over her mouth. She began to struggle violently, but the extra strength she had gained in her arms was no match for my power, which was now infinite. Time stood still for me then, and I have no idea how long it was before her frenzied efforts began to subside – a minute perhaps, maybe two. Finally, her writhing tailed off and then ceased, but I continued to lie over her lifeless body, probably for several minutes, my own body as limp as my mind.

I can remember little of what happened then. I do recall standing for a while, numbly looking down at the terrible scene on the bed. But the journey home remains a murky collection of emotions and feelings —

grief, fear, panic, but also the chill of the water as I swam home.

Chapter 25

I awoke in my own bed. The oppressive clouds of apprehension immediately rolled back in as memories of the previous day's horrific events flooded into my mind. I felt utterly crushed, and went about my morning routine in a daze, all the time expecting the police to arrive. Would it be a couple of raps on the door perhaps, or would a SWAT team burst through with guns drawn?

I was already resigned to facing the full retribution of the law and, as I silently forced down a meagre breakfast, I succumbed to a dense cocktail of morbid sounds and images — the rasp of the ratchets as I was handcuffed, the secure clank as my cell door was slammed shut, bumpy rides in prison vans, long hours alone in cells, various courtrooms, culminating in my trial for murder and the foreman of the jury stepping forward to announce their verdict of guilty. And then the Judge as he began to deliver his sentence, "most heinous crime I have ever encountered", "poor defenceless girl, confined to a wheelchair." I paused briefly, wondering whether Italy had kept the death penalty and if so, what form would my execution take — the guillotine perhaps.

Only gradually did my mind begin to greet the new day with any breath of clarity, for I have frequently woken to such horrors in times of stress, and soon began to recognise the pattern. Had it all been some terrible dream perhaps? The empty bottle of whiskey bore evidence of my previous night's condition and planted seeds of doubt in my mind, upon which I pounced eagerly.

I began to search for inconsistencies in my memory of the events that might prove I was no murderer. I looked for signs of blood on my body and clothes but soon realised that the long swim home would have washed away all traces. And would the Barone have scurried so readily to her assistance? Recalling our meeting, it seemed very unlikely he would ever wish to meet with her again.

But above all, was I actually capable of such actions? No one had lived in our little house in Italy for many years before we bought it, and flies had taken occupation. We installed a battery of measures to combat the problem, including sprays and sticky paper rolls. More aggressively, I purchased a plastic swat whose unique feature was a hole, the shape of a fly in flight, cut into one corner of the mesh. As I whack it, I like to believe that this hole gives the fly a sporting chance to escape, although I have yet to see one take advantage of it. I have no qualms about killing flies when they become a nuisance, but I wouldn't wish to hurt one unnecessarily. Nor have I ever killed an animal, even the badger that caused my father so much grief when it tore up his lawn. And I don't recall ever seriously hitting anyone – even in anger. I find it difficult to conceive of damaging, let alone killing, a fellow human being.

Maybe I was fooling myself, but the cruel clouds were soon beginning to lift, and with no police arriving at my doorstep, I began to convince myself that the whole episode had indeed been just another of my appalling nightmares. Over the following days and nights, my conviction hardened, with my heart only occasionally missing a beat or two at a ring from the telephone.

With the comfort this brought, I slowly began to plan my future. I needed to get away from Italy, for a while at least and left for home. But I had already set off before it hit me . . . where exactly was home? For one fleeting moment, I had visions of arriving at Angie's door but, like my father in Norfolk, she belonged to a previous life. With a rising sense of excitement, mingled with a degree of apprehension, I began to look forward to my new life, free of marriage, free of Selene — full of fresh opportunities.

As I drove, I pondered the trail of events that had led to the last of my days with Selene. Was she the terrible ogre I had uncovered at our last meeting? I found myself with considerable sympathy for her plight. Other than her exceptional looks, was she not a girl like any other, making her way in life as best she could? The fates had conspired to consign her to an endless procession of liaisons such as ours, each destined to end badly. I had set her up as my goddess and placed her on a most precarious pedestal, doubtless fashioned from the ruins of my marriage to Angie. Surely, it was wholly unsurprising that the entire edifice had been eventually toppled, with her mortality cruelly exposed.

I checked into the hotel I had used before. Realising I would need a more permanent base, I immediately set local agents to work, and it was only a few days before I was networking amongst my old cronies. I was encouraged to find that my previous site foreman had got wind of a possible development scheme. It may come to nothing, of course, but the very thought has reignited that old feeling of excitement in my stomach.

I have not tried to get in touch with Selene and, as far as I am aware, she has never attempted to find me. I am not even certain as to whether she is alive or dead. But, to echo the sentiments of her Italian Baron, and Rhett Butler before him, "*I really don't give a damn.*"

I recall my early morning flight from the island in the company of the amazing blood moon. To the ancient Greeks, Selene was a goddess of that moon – my father had taught me that. I had spent a full year basking in the brilliance that radiated from her. As it had waned, it continued to glow for a while, but had finally disappeared on that fateful night and I have now put the yearlong adventure firmly behind me.

Memories of Julie drifted into my mind the other day. We had parted abruptly, and I was curious as to how things had worked out for her. I remembered that I still had her number on my mobile, but there was no reply.

This immediately set up visions of her in Australia, reconciled with her Brad, but I left a message to give me a ring sometime.

A couple of days later, as I was working on my new project, I did get a call and approached the phone with visions of Julie at the other end. But disappointment came swiftly, as a man's voice began with an abrupt, "Signor Ramsay?"

I was shaken as I instantly recognised the heavy Italian accent. I must have paused a mite too long because the voice came again, "Signor Ramsay?"

My heart leapt. What could the Ispettore want of me?

"Signor Ramsay? It is Ispettore Grimaldi here. Can you hear me?"

My heart was racing but I managed a nervous, "Good morning, Ispettore. How are you?"

"I am well thank you", he replied briefly. After a short pause, he continued, "May I ask, have you visited your house in Italy recently?"

"I was out there for a while. I came back to England a few weeks ago. Why do you ask?"

"There has been an incident at The House on the Lake."

I froze at the bald simplicity of the statement — an incident? I was unable to speak for several seconds.

"I see," I responded eventually. "What sort of an incident?"

"Murder," announced Grimaldi, as tersely as before. "A double murder — two people you knew. At the moment, it seems they killed one another."

I could say nothing then. I sat staring silently at the phone.

"Signore Ramsay?"

I remained silent.

"Signore Ramsay? Are you there?"

Printed in Great Britain
by Amazon